"She's not our baby."

Ruston stared at Gracelyn, trying to figure out if she was telling him the truth.

"Abigail's not my baby either."

"Then whose child is she? Because she looks like you." He stopped. "Is she Allie's? Is she your niece?"

Gracelyn nodded. "Those people running the baby farm were still after us. And I couldn't stay a cop. So I planned on...running. Hiding."

"You could have come to me."

"No, I couldn't. You still trusted the cops. I didn't. I knew you weren't dirty, but someone blew our cover, someone who could have been another cop."

"How'd you end up with Allie's baby?"

"She showed up shortly after I turned in my badge, scared. She told me she was pregnant and her boyfriend was abusive. So I took her with me. Allie gave birth to Abigail eight weeks ago in Houston. Then she disappeared, leaving me a note, asking me to take care of Abigail. She wanted to try to make amends with Abigail's biological dad, Devin Blackburn. He's bad news, Ruston."

PROTECTING THE NEWBORN

USA TODAY BESTSELLING AUTHOR
DELORES FOSSEN

Harlequin
INTRIGUE

Harlequin®
INTRIGUE™

ISBN-13: 978-1-335-45702-8

Protecting the Newborn

Copyright © 2024 by Delores Fossen

Recycling programs
for this product may
not exist in your area.

Harlequin Enterprises ULC
22 Adelaide St. West, 41st Floor
Toronto, Ontario M5H 4E3, Canada
www.Harlequin.com

Printed in U.S.A.

Delores Fossen, a *USA TODAY* bestselling author, has written over a hundred and fifty novels, with millions of copies of her books in print worldwide. She's received a Booksellers' Best Award and an RT Reviewers' Choice Best Book Award. She was also a finalist for a prestigious RITA® Award. You can contact the author through her website at www.deloresfossen.com.

Books by Delores Fossen

Harlequin Intrigue

Saddle Ridge Justice

The Sheriff's Baby
Protecting the Newborn

Silver Creek Lawman: Second Generation

Targeted in Silver Creek
Maverick Detective Dad
Last Seen in Silver Creek
Marked for Revenge

The Law in Lubbock County

Sheriff in the Saddle
Maverick Justice
Lawman to the Core
Spurred to Justice

Visit the Author Profile page at Harlequin.com.

CAST OF CHARACTERS

Detective Ruston McCullough—While undercover, he's hired to kidnap his former partner and a newborn, but when the situation turns deadly, Ruston is forced to take them into hiding to protect them.

Gracelyn Wallace—A former cop whose last assignment may be responsible for the danger that's happening now. She has no choice but to trust Ruston so they can work together to save the baby Gracelyn loves.

Abigail Wallace—Gracelyn's infant niece, who was abandoned by her biological mom. Gracelyn and Ruston will do whatever it takes to keep her safe.

Allie Wallace—She gave birth to Abigail, but she's a danger to both herself and the baby.

Devin Blackburn—Allie's ex-boyfriend who not only has a police record but also criminal ties. He could be responsible for the attempts to kill Gracelyn and Ruston.

Charla Burke—An undercover detective who might be willing to do anything to cover up her past.

Tony Franklin—A high-ranking cop who could be dirty. Is he pulling the strings to try to have Ruston and Gracelyn killed?

Chapter One

Staying behind the cover of some sprawling oak trees, Detective Ruston McCullough pressed the night-vision binoculars to his eyes and got his first look of the place.

His target's house.

It was one story with a white stone exterior and was positioned dead smack in the middle of about three acres. Woods and old ranch trails formed a horseshoe around the house and the pasture.

Lots of places for someone to lie in wait.

Lots of places for a kidnapper or killer to hide.

Once, the house had belonged to a rancher and his wife, both now deceased, and their heirs rented out the place. The current renter, Lizzy Martin, had been living there for a little less than a month.

And she was Ruston's target.

Well, she would have been the target if he truly was a scumbag thug hired to kidnap the woman and her baby. He wasn't. He was an undercover San Antonio PD detective posing as a scumbag thug, but the slime who'd hired him didn't know that.

The slime, aka Marty Bennett, believed that Ruston was a dishonorably discharged army combat specialist with a rap sheet for assault who would do the job that Marty had hired him to do. That Ruston would kidnap the woman and baby and then bring them to Marty, so the baby could probably be sold on the black market and the woman could likely become a human-trafficking victim.

Ruston wouldn't be doing that.

No way.

Once he had the kid and woman secure and out of any harm's way, Ruston's fellow officers would move in to take Marty into custody at his San Antonio residence. Then Ruston would start creating another undercover persona while other detectives figured out for certain why Marty wanted this particular woman. Trafficking and the black market were always good guesses in situations like this.

But something about that theory didn't feel right.

If those were indeed Marty's motives, then Ruston wondered how the heck Marty had even seen her and the baby. This place in rural Texas wasn't on any beaten path, and judging from the gossip Ruston had picked up from his moles and snitches about this Lizzy Martin, no one had seen her in any of the nearby towns.

All three of those towns, including his own hometown of Saddle Ridge, were plenty small enough that folks would have recalled a stranger, especially one with a newborn baby. Added to that, he had siblings in law enforcement in Saddle Ridge, and neither of them had seen anyone resembling the description he had of Lizzy Martin.

Marty hadn't given Ruston a photo of the woman. Only her name, address and a few skimpy details. She was supposedly around five and a half feet tall, average build, brown hair and brown eyes. Considering that could apply to many women, Ruston had decided to run a background check on her—a skill set his undercover persona wouldn't have had, so Ruston had had to cover his tracks there in case Marty was monitoring him.

It had taken a while for Ruston to weed through all the possibilities with the name variations for Lizzy Martin, but he thought the one who had rented this place was a website designer who worked from home. Her driver's license photo showed a woman who was indeed as average as Marty's description of her. It seemed to Ruston that Lizzy was actually trying to fade into the background of that DMV photo. That was a lot to assume from a picture, but it had put him on further alert.

People who tried to hide usually had a reason for doing so.

That was why he'd come to the house earlier than planned. Ruston had told Marty that he would take the target at midnight, but he'd arrived four hours before that with the hopes that he'd catch a glimpse of her.

So far, he hadn't.

But someone was definitely inside the house, because he'd seen lights go on and off.

The breeze rustled through the trees around him, and he welcomed the somewhat cooler night air. It was late June, but in central Texas, it could still be scalding hot even at this time of night. Proof of that was the line of sweat already trickling down his back.

Ruston shifted the binoculars when he caught some movement in the front window. It was indeed a woman, and while he couldn't see her face, since she had her back to him, her height and hair color fit Marty's description. He watched as she picked up something.

A baby monitor.

She peered down at a little screen that he saw light up. The binoculars weren't clear enough for him to see the baby she was watching, but he could make out the outline of a crib on the screen.

Ruston continued to watch until she moved out of sight. A few seconds later, he saw the light go on in the front right window. Probably a bedroom or an office. Since he had verification she was indeed there, it was showtime.

Putting away his binoculars, Ruston eased out from the cover of the trees, and he crouched down to make his way closer to the house. He kept watch, looking and listening for anything or anybody, but the only sounds were an owl, some cicadas and the soft drumming of his own heartbeat in his ears.

He stayed low, not going toward that window with the light since he didn't want Lizzy to see him and then call the cops. Because there was a child on the premises, the locals would likely respond fast, and word of that could get back to Marty if he had his own moles and snitches in law enforcement. Ruston didn't want Marty to have a clue this was a sting operation until he had the woman and baby someplace safe.

Keeping up his slow and steady pace, Ruston went toward the back of the house, figuring he would first scope out all sides to see if there was an easy point of entry. He didn't like breaking in, but that was his best bet. Then he could sneak up on her, and before she could make that call to the locals, he could convince her that he was a cop and was there to help.

He stopped at the back corner of the house, peered around it. And because of the dim light coming from the porch, he saw the gun.

It was pointed right at his face.

He automatically drew his own gun. His body jolted, flooding with adrenaline, and he was ready to fight, to get that gun, but then he saw the face of the woman holding it. Not Lizzy and damn sure not the face of the woman in the driver's license. However, it was someone he instantly recognized.

"Gracelyn Wallace," he snapped.

His former partner at SAPD, and a woman he hadn't seen in nearly a year. Correction—a woman he'd been trying to find for ten and a half months. He sure as heck hadn't expected to find her here.

But she had obviously expected to see him.

There wasn't any surprise in her expression, just a steely anger. And some fear. Yeah, she couldn't mask that completely.

Her looks had changed plenty since he'd last laid eyes on her. No short, choppy blond hair but rather the shoulder-length brown that fit the description Marty had given him. Her face was thinner, as if she'd lost weight. And while she sort of resembled the photo on her driver's license, it was obvious that was a fake.

"What are you doing here?" Ruston demanded, though he was pretty sure that was a question she'd been about to ask him.

Her crystal green eyes narrowed even more. "I'm trying to stay alive," she snarled.

He hadn't been sure how she would answer, but Ruston hadn't expected that. "Alive?" he repeated. "Who's trying to kill you?"

Gracelyn huffed, lowered her gun. "Well, I guess it's not you." She tipped her head to the eaves of the house. "I didn't see anyone else with you. Are you alone?"

He glanced up at the eaves, and while it was too dark to spot a camera, one was obviously there. Hell. Whatever was going on, this was not the easy snatch and grab that Marty had said it would be.

"I'm alone," he assured her, "and you're in danger. But I'm guessing you already know that if you have cameras."

"I have cameras and perimeter security. You tripped one of the sensors, and my phone immediately gave me an alert." She made an uneasy glance around them. "Tell me why you're here and then leave. I don't have time for a long explanation."

Ruston mentally replayed each word. That was a lot of security for someone who was no longer a cop. It was more of a setup that a criminal would have. Or someone scared to the bone.

He was going with door number two on this.

And he thought he knew why.

Over ten months ago, Gracelyn and he had had the undercover mission from hell. Deep-cover infiltration of what was basically a baby farm. A place where pregnant women had been held and then their babies had been sold. Some of the women hadn't been there voluntarily either. Many were runaways who'd been scooped up by the SOBs who'd set up the operation. Others were illegal immigrants. Some were victims of human trafficking.

The operation hadn't been sloppy or easy to break into, but Gracelyn and he had managed it by being hired as security guards. They'd been in the facility for less than twenty-four hours and had managed to get absolutely nothing on the person or persons running the place when they realized their covers had been blown. That had become crystal clear when thugs had come into their quarters to murder them. They'd managed to escape, barely, but had then ended up in a seedy motel together, waiting for some fellow undercover cops to come and get them.

Ruston had a lot of nightmarish memories of that night.

And some memories that weren't of the nightmare variety.

Before that night, there had always been an attraction between Gracelyn and him. Always the heat.

Which they'd resisted because they were partners.

But they hadn't resisted enough after nearly being killed. They'd landed in bed, and a couple of hours later, when they'd been safely taken back to headquarters in San Antonio, Gracelyn had put in her resignation papers and had disappeared.

Ruston had not only looked for her, but he'd also continued to hunt for the person who'd run the baby farm. He'd ended up needing to hunt for the farm itself, too, since they'd moved locations. Of course they had. If the powers that be had figured out Gracelyn and he were cops, they would have known the place was no longer safe for their operation.

"I haven't been able to find the baby farm," he admitted. "You're worried about them coming after you?"

"And you're not?" she countered.

"I look over my shoulder a lot," he muttered, doing that now. He didn't like being out in the open like this. Even with all her security, that didn't mean someone couldn't gun them down.

"I have a new undercover identity," Ruston explained. "One that has no connections to the assignment we had together. But I've closely monitored the old identities we used, and there aren't any red flags." In other words, no one was searching for them under those names.

"Then why are you here?" Gracelyn's tone was nowhere close to being friendly.

Since Ruston didn't want to stand around outside any

longer, he just spilled it. "Someone hired me to kidnap you. You and the baby who's living here with you."

But then he paused. And did some thinking. Or rather some calculating.

"The baby who's living here with you," he repeated. "How old is he or she?" Because that was a detail that Marty hadn't given him. And it could be critical information, since Gracelyn and he had had sex ten and a half months ago.

Hell.

Was the child his?

"She's a newborn," Gracelyn muttered, her words rushing out as if to put a stop to the shock that must have been on his face. "She's only two weeks old."

Two weeks. So, the timing didn't fit. "She's your baby?" He had to ask because something else occurred to him.

That maybe Gracelyn had gotten the child from someone. Maybe from a baby farm or someone needing to put the baby in a safe place. That wouldn't explain why Marty had wanted the child kidnapped, though. But there were a lot of things that needed explaining right now.

"She's mine," Gracelyn finally said, but she didn't elaborate. However, she did take out something from the pocket of her jogging pants. The baby monitor he'd seen her looking at when she'd been by the window.

"Let's go inside and talk," he insisted. "Because something's wrong. I'm not sure what, but we need to figure out why someone hired me to kidnap you and the newborn."

She didn't jump at his request, but after another glance at the monitor, she motioned for him to follow her. Gracelyn still had her gun gripped in her hand, and even though it was no longer pointed at him, she didn't put it away.

Gracelyn led him into a small kitchen that at first glance seemed ordinary, with its outdated appliances and flowery wallpaper. Then he saw a tablet-sized device on the counter, and there were four images on the split screen that showed camera feed from all four sides of the house.

"Yeah," he remarked, "you would have seen me coming on that."

She made a sound of agreement and finally slipped her gun into what he realized was a slide holster in the back of her pants. She then triple locked the back door, took out her phone and showed him the same footage that was on the laptop.

"I get an alert if a camera or perimeter sensor is triggered," she explained.

"That's a lot of security," Ruston muttered, holstering his own gun. "Want to tell me why you need it?"

Gracelyn glanced away, murmuring something under her breath that Ruston didn't catch. "You might not have been tracked by anyone from our last mission, but I believe I have been. If not someone from the mission, then someone else."

Everything inside him went still. "What do you mean?"

She dragged in a long breath and kept her attention pinned to the baby monitor. "About a month after I resigned from SAPD, I was renting a place in Dallas, and I wasn't using my real name. It wasn't the same identity I'd used in the undercover op either, and I was being careful. *Very.* Anyway, I realized someone was following me. I set up cameras and got proof of it. I couldn't see his face, but he was definitely tracking me."

Ruston cursed. "Was it a tall, lanky guy about six feet, sandy-blond hair and chin scruff?" he asked.

That got her gaze shifting back to him. "No. Dark hair, about six foot three, muscular build. Why? Who's the guy you just described?"

"Marty Bennett, the lowlife who hired me to kidnap you and your baby." Now Ruston needed a long, deep breath. "I figured it was for trafficking or a black-market adoption. But maybe not," he added in a grumble.

Maybe Marty had a much bigger part in this.

One that had involved following Gracelyn long before he'd hired Ruston. But if Marty had known where she was all this time, why hadn't he taken her before now?

"Tell me about this Marty Bennett," Gracelyn insisted. "Is he connected in any way to the baby farm?"

Ruston shook his head. "Nothing in his background indicates that, and I dug hard and deep on him. Everything points to him being a somewhat successful money launderer and embezzler. He's got gambling debts, so I figured he somehow found out about you and the baby and thought he could earn some quick cash."

She didn't say anything, but he saw the muscles tighten in her face. Heard the shudder of breath she released. Gracelyn was worried and scared.

"Has anyone else followed you since you moved here?" he asked.

"Not that I know of, but I've moved twice since leaving that apartment in Dallas. I was within a week of leaving here because it doesn't feel safe to stay in one place for long."

Ruston wanted to curse again. And pull her into his arms. Not because of the heat, though that was still there. No, he wanted to try to ease some of that fear. But after what had happened between them, he seriously doubted a hug from him would give her much comfort.

"What about your sister, Allie?" he asked. "Does she know where you are?"

Allie was the only family Gracelyn had. Well, other than

the baby. And while Allie and Gracelyn hadn't been especially close, just the opposite actually, anyone wanting to get to Gracelyn could use Allie to do it. Allie had been pretty much a screwup most of her life, and Gracelyn had had to pull strings and call in favors several times to get her kid sister out of a jam.

"Allie doesn't know," Gracelyn answered, and then she swallowed hard. "And I don't know where she is either." She paused. "I'm not sure if she's safe or not."

Hell. Of course, she'd be worried about Allie. Worried about someone using her sister to get to her.

"You should have gotten in touch with me," he said. "You should have told me. I could have helped."

She laughed, but there was no humor in it. It was dry as West Texas dust. "Right. The man with one of the most dangerous jobs on the planet. The last person I wanted to contact was you."

Ruston's stomach twisted. But he couldn't deny what she'd just said. That last op they'd been on together, the one that had nearly gotten them killed, had obviously sent them in opposite directions. He'd kept up the deep-cover work, and she'd chosen to make her world as safe as possible. The pregnancy and the baby had no doubt factored into her lifestyle decisions.

And that brought him back to her newborn.

Two weeks old, which meant Gracelyn had hooked up with her baby's father six or seven weeks after she'd resigned from the force. Since they'd been partners, Ruston knew plenty about Gracelyn's personal life. And vice versa. She hadn't been involved with anyone when they'd had their one-off, and even though that night had been the culmination of the worst of circumstances, he'd thought it would be the beginning of a relationship since there'd always been an intense attraction between them.

Clearly, he'd been wrong about the relationship.

But not wrong about the attraction. It was still there, even now. Or maybe he was reading way too much into it. After all, Gracelyn had been with her baby's father roughly nine and a half months ago, which meant that was a month after Ruston and she had had that one night together.

"Is your baby's father in the picture?" he asked. Ruston watched her face to see if that was playing into this. Relationships went south all the time, and this man could be the threat to Gracelyn and her daughter.

It seemed to him that she tensed even more. Something he hadn't thought possible. After a long pause, Gracelyn opened her mouth but didn't get a chance to answer.

Because of the soft beeping sound.

Her gaze flew from his and went to the laptop monitor. "Someone or something just triggered the security alarm."

Chapter Two

Every nerve in Gracelyn's body was already on high alert, but that little beep of her security system gave her a fresh surge of adrenaline. She cursed herself for not having already moved. If she had, then the nightmare wouldn't have found her.

Maybe Ruston wouldn't have found her either.

She'd have to deal with him. But first, she had to handle this threat that could put the baby, Abigail, in danger.

While she hurried through a mental checklist of her security, Gracelyn went closer to the laptop monitor. She already knew all the windows and the doors were locked, and that every possible point of entry was equipped with sensors.

It hadn't been any of those that'd gone off, though.

That would have been a much louder beep. This softer sound had been because someone or something had moved past one of the sensors set up around the entire perimeter of the house.

She glanced through the various camera feeds and soon spotted the culprit, and she relaxed just a little. "A deer," she muttered. "There are dozens of them around, and they often set off the sensors."

Ruston moved closer to her, looking at the laptop screen as well. So close that she caught his scent. It stirred through her in a totally different way than the adrenaline and nerves.

A bad way.

Because it reminded her of the heat between them.

Reminded her of why they'd landed in bed. That couldn't happen again. Still, it was hard not to notice that face, that body that had drawn her to him in the first place. Ruston was very much the cowboy cop, though his dark brown hair was longer than most cops'. The length was no doubt to go along with his undercover persona. Ditto for the scruff that made him look like an Old West outlaw.

She kept her attention on the screen, looking for anyone or anything else that the deer's movements could have masked. When she'd set up the security, it had occurred to her that an intruder could sneak in behind a deer or some other animal, so she always looked for that. Always.

The seconds crawled by, turning into minutes, and she still didn't see any signs of an intruder. Gracelyn couldn't breathe easier, though. Not with Ruston standing next to her. She had to get rid of him fast so she could get out of there with the baby.

"I read about what happened to your father," she said to jump-start the conversation. Jump-start and then finish it as soon as she got any and all info from him.

He nodded, and she saw the pain flood his cool gray eyes. Pain because his father, Cliff, had been murdered seven months earlier. Gunned down by an unknown assailant. Since his dad had also been the sheriff of Saddle Ridge, Texas, the speculation around his murder centered on his investigations.

And his wife.

Sandra McCullough had left Saddle Ridge just hours before her husband's murder, and she hadn't returned. Of course, Ruston and his siblings, who were all lawmen, wanted to find her. To question her, too. But there was also the fear that she couldn't be found because she was dead. Or because she'd had some part in her husband's death and was now on the run.

"Among other things, your father was investigating the kidnapping of two pregnant women," Gracelyn continued. "According to what I've read, he thought that maybe the kidnappings were possibly connected to the baby farm where we were nearly killed." She stopped and waited for him to confirm or deny that.

Ruston was clearly still working through the horrible memories of losing his father and his missing mother, but he finally nodded. "He was investigating that. What no one has been able to do is link his murder to that case."

"Do you believe there's a link?" she came out and asked.

He didn't get a chance to answer though because his phone vibrated in his pocket. Ruston frowned when he looked at the caller. "It's Marty."

She didn't have to encourage Ruston to take the call. He wanted answers just as much as she did, and this Marty just might be able to give them some. It sickened her though to have to deal with the devil, but Gracelyn was willing to do whatever it took to keep the baby safe.

"Yeah," Ruston said when he answered, and he put the call on speaker. A sign that he had likely been up-front as to why he was here and had nothing to hide.

Unlike her.

Gracelyn wanted those answers. Desperately wanted them. But she also had to get Ruston out of there.

"Steve," the caller said, obviously calling Ruston by his cover name, "I need you to move things up. Get out to the woman's place right now and take her and the kid."

That tightened every muscle in her body. Judging from

the way Ruston pulled back his shoulders, he was having a similar reaction.

"Why?" Ruston asked. "What's wrong?"

"I just need her sooner than expected. I've had to work around some transportation issues."

Marty had said that so calmly, all business. There was no hint that he even thought of her and Abigail as anything more than objects.

"Transportation issues," Ruston repeated. "Am I still supposed to take her and the baby to the warehouse in San Antonio?"

"You are, but the people picking her up want her there earlier than planned. Make it happen," Marty insisted.

People. So, maybe Marty was just the middleman on this. Still, middlemen often knew who'd hired them.

"You didn't say, but why do you want this particular woman?" Ruston pressed.

"That's none of your business," Marty snapped, punctuating that with some profanity. "I didn't pay you to ask questions. If you can't take the woman and the kid, then I'll send someone else to do the job, and you'll pay me back every penny of the advance I gave you."

Gracelyn figured that wouldn't be all, that Marty would try to silence Ruston so he wouldn't blow the whistle on him.

"I said I'll get her and the baby and I will." Ruston's voice was a snap, too. "It just makes me uneasy when plans change. I don't want to grab them, show up at the warehouse and then have nobody there waiting to take them off my hands."

"Somebody will be waiting there for you," Marty growled. "Now, get them and finish this." With that barked order, Marty ended the call.

Ruston stared at the phone a few seconds and shook his

head. "I'd planned on dropping you and your baby at a safe house and then driving out to the warehouse with decoys."

Gracelyn had been so shocked at Ruston's arrival that she hadn't had a chance to ask him how he'd planned for all of this to play out. "Decoys?" she questioned.

He nodded. "Charla Burke," he said, referring to an SAPD detective they'd both worked with. "And a dummy baby. Obviously, Charla and I would both be armed, and we'd planned on arresting whoever was waiting in that warehouse. Other cops would be moving to take Marty at the same time." He paused a heartbeat. "I need to let Franklin know about this."

Lieutenant Tony Franklin, the senior officer in charge of undercover assignments in the SAPD Special Victims Unit. Gracelyn didn't have any reason to distrust Franklin or Charla, but she didn't care for them knowing her current location. Then again, Marty obviously knew, too, which meant heaven knew how many others did as well.

Yes, it was definitely well past time for her to leave.

"I have my own safe house already in place," Gracelyn said, and it got the reaction from Ruston that she expected.

His forehead bunched up, and he huffed. Obviously, he knew she could handle herself—most of the time, anyway—but he was probably still concerned. Heck, so was she.

"I don't want police protection," Gracelyn spelled out to him and left it at that.

No need for her to remind him that being a cop hadn't helped either of them on their last assignment. Yes, they'd both gotten out of there alive, barely, but that'd been more luck than training. At least two dozen bullets had been fired at them during their escape, and they'd received only minor injuries.

Well, minor *physical* injuries, anyway.

Gracelyn was still living with the nightmare of nearly being gunned down, and she figured it was the same for Ruston. Except Ruston had been able to go back to the job. She hadn't been.

A soft sound shot through the room. Not the security system this time, but a kitten-like cry that had come from the baby monitor. Gracelyn immediately looked and saw Abigail was squirming in her crib. That was her cue to get Ruston moving.

"You can leave now," she insisted, going to the bottom drawer beneath the stove and pulling out a go bag that had cash, fake IDs and a gun. She already had other supplies stashed in her SUV in the garage.

Ruston didn't budge. "I hate to see you on your own like this. I know you don't trust me, but I can help you."

She was ready to assure him that she didn't need his help, but the baby's fussing turned into a full cry. Gracelyn checked her watch, even though she knew it wasn't time for a bottle. She'd fed Abigail less than a half hour before Ruston had arrived.

"I'll be fine," Gracelyn said, and she hoped that was true.

She'd been so careful, and here at least four other people knew her current location. Ruston, Marty, Lieutenant Franklin and Charla. Soon, Gracelyn would want to dig into how Marty and his cohorts had found her. And why he wanted her and Abigail. For now, though, she had to move.

When the crying went up a significant notch, Gracelyn hooked the go bag over her shoulder and headed to the nursery. "I'll get Abigail and leave. Goodbye, Ruston."

"Abigail," he repeated. "You named her after your late mother."

She nodded. Then scowled when he followed her. "No need for you to lock up when you go," she insisted, stopping outside the nursery door to stare at him. "I'll be out of here within minutes."

Ruston stared back. And stared. Then he muttered some profanity under his breath, reached around her and opened the nursery door. He maneuvered around her before she could stop him, and he made a beeline to the crib.

Gracelyn's heart went to her knees.

Somehow, she managed to get her legs working, and she hurried to scoop up the baby. But not before Ruston got a good look at her.

Ruston didn't say anything for several long moments, and even though the only illumination in the room was from a night-light, Gracelyn saw his jaw muscles turn to iron.

"Abigail isn't two weeks old," he said, his voice a low, dangerous snarl.

"No. She's eight weeks old." And Gracelyn quickly tacked on a huge detail that Ruston needed to hear. "She's not our baby."

Ruston had already opened his mouth, no doubt to accuse her of not telling him that he'd gotten her pregnant, but her comment stopped him. Temporarily, anyway. He stared at her, and stared, clearly trying to figure out if she was telling him the truth.

She was.

"Abigail's not my baby either," she added.

Again, Ruston had clearly been gearing up to accuse her of all sorts of things that she wouldn't have done. Yes, she was desperate. Still was. But if she'd had Ruston's baby, she would have figured out a way to tell him about it.

"Then whose child is she?" he demanded. "Because she looks like you." He stopped again. "Is she Allie's? Is she your niece?"

Gracelyn nodded. Of course, that confirmation was

going to lead to a whole bunch of other questions. Questions that she couldn't answer. Still, she was going to have to give Ruston something or he'd never leave. Best to start at the beginning, which ironically had been at the end of her career as a cop.

"We didn't catch those people who were running the baby farm," she went on. "They were after us, and I couldn't dissolve into the background by taking on another undercover persona. Because I couldn't be a cop. So, I planned on…running. Hiding. Staying safe."

"You could have come to me," he insisted.

"No, I couldn't have." It was a truth that was going to cut him to the bone, but he had to hear it. "You still trusted the cops. I didn't. I knew you weren't dirty, but someone blew our cover at that baby farm, and that someone could have been another cop."

That was a reminder for her to get out of there with Abigail, since two cops she wasn't 100 percent certain she could trust—Charla and Lieutenant Franklin—knew her location. Well, they knew the location of Lizzy Martin, anyway. But it was possible that they knew it was an alias she'd been using.

"How'd you end up with Allie's baby?" Ruston asked.

Gracelyn gathered the long breath that she'd need. "Allie showed up shortly after I turned in my badge, just as I was about to go on the run. She was scared." And sporting a black eye and bruises on her arms. "She told me her boyfriend was abusive. And that she'd just taken a pregnancy test and was about two or three weeks pregnant. So, I took Allie with me."

She'd had no choice about that. Allie could be flighty and restless, but there was no way Gracelyn could have abandoned the child and her.

"Using an alias I'd set up for her, Allie gave birth to

Abigail eight weeks ago in Houston," Gracelyn went on. "Then, a week later, Allie disappeared. She left me a note, asking me to take care of Abigail, but that she wanted to try to make amends with Abigail's bio-dad, Devin Blackburn. He's bad news, Ruston."

She didn't get into the details of that, but Devin Blackburn had money and connections—and three restraining orders from previous relationships. He'd been arrested twice for assault and computer hacking, but the money and connections had kept him from doing any time in a cage.

However, there was one connection Ruston needed to know about. Except she could tell from his expression that he'd already figured it out.

"Devin Blackburn," he repeated. "He was one of the names that came up during the baby-farm investigation."

She nodded. There'd been dozens involved in that case, maybe hundreds, but Devin's name had popped up because he had known associations with a baby broker who'd worked for the farm. Since that particular broker had turned up dead, the cops hadn't been able to learn if Devin's association had led to anything criminal.

"I obviously couldn't risk Allie bringing Devin to the house in Houston, because I didn't know who else he'd let know I was there, so I brought Abigail here," Gracelyn added. "I keep a burner phone and a private Facebook account that Allie could have used to get in touch with me so I could let her know where I was." She paused. Had to. "But she hasn't contacted me, and I haven't been able to get in touch with her."

He shook his head. "If you'd come to me, I could have helped keep Allie, you and the baby safe," he insisted.

"You would have tried, but it would have meant giving up your badge," she insisted right back. "All four of us would have been in hiding until the people responsible for the danger are caught." She paused again, then drew in a long breath. "I think I'm close to finding those people."

That got his attention, and his glare morphed into a puzzled look. "Who? Is it Marty?"

She shook her head. "I don't have names. I have computer identities that I found on a website that's basically an auction site for babies. One of the identities is Green Eagle."

Gracelyn didn't have to explain why that was important. Ruston would recall it was what the person running the baby farm had called himself or herself.

"That can't be a coincidence," she added.

He made a sound that could have meant anything. Ruston certainly didn't jump to agree to that. "I looked for leaks in SAPD. For any signs that someone had ratted us out. I found nothing."

Gracelyn had known he would look, and if he had indeed found the culprit—if there was a dirty cop to find, that was—Ruston would have already told her.

"I did what I believed was necessary to keep Abigail safe," Gracelyn went on. "And if I had learned the identity of Green Eagle, I'd planned to contact you and give you the name so you could arrest him or her."

He went quiet again, but his gaze stayed intense. "We're going to talk more about Abigail and Allie," he said like a demand. "But for now, I want to know everything you have on Green Eagle and the baby auction."

She nodded. "Not here, though," she said and would have reminded him that it was too dangerous to stay here.

A sound stopped her.

It was that punch-to-the-gut beep from her security system, and even though it was possibly another deer, she whipped out her phone from her pocket and looked at the screen.

The slam of adrenaline knocked the breath out of her.

Because it wasn't a deer. In the milky haze of moonlight, Gracelyn saw the shadowy figure coming straight toward the house.

Chapter Three

Even though Gracelyn didn't say anything, Ruston instantly knew from the change in her body language that something was wrong.

She thrust out her phone screen so he could see what had put that alarm on her face. One look at the person in dark clothes, and Ruston was certain he was sporting plenty of alarm of his own.

He drew his gun and braced for an attack.

Ruston also took a harder look at the intruder to see if he recognized him, but he couldn't see the person's face because it was covered with a mask. He couldn't even be sure if it was a man or woman. He definitely couldn't rule out this being Marty. Or one of his hired guns.

But if Marty had come after him like this, then why not just take him when they'd had their initial meeting? They'd been alone for that with no obvious witnesses. Why wait until Ruston was here?

Unless both Gracelyn and he were targets.

Or maybe the target was the baby.

If so, that pointed right back to the baby farm and this mystery person, Green Eagle. And unfortunately, it could point right back to Ruston himself.

"I was careful," Ruston muttered to Gracelyn. "I didn't see anyone following me here."

That didn't mean, though, that someone hadn't managed to tail him. That caused him to mentally curse. Because, hell, everything about this could have been a setup.

"The windows aren't bulletproof," she whispered, grabbing a blanket from the chair next to the crib.

Gracelyn scooped up the baby, automatically trying to soothe her with gentle rocking motions and murmurs. A necessity, since any sound would alert an intruder to their specific location in the house.

"I have to get her to my SUV," Gracelyn added.

Gracelyn didn't invite Ruston to come along, but he did anyway. He had no intention of letting them out of his sight.

"Are the windows of your SUV bullet resistant?" he asked, following her out of the nursery.

"They are," Gracelyn answered, hurrying into the hall.

She had her hands full, literally, what with holding both the phone and Abigail. Plus, she had a backpack hooked over her shoulder, but she waved off Ruston when he tried to help her.

They'd barely made it another step, though, when they heard the sound. Definitely not something Ruston wanted to hear either.

A gunshot blasted through one the windows.

Ruston muttered some profanity and stepped in front of Gracelyn and the baby. They hunkered down seconds before the next shot. There was the sound of shattering glass falling on the floor, but Ruston didn't see any bullets coming through the wall near them.

"Give me your phone," he insisted. "I can see if he's alone and if he's using any kind of infrared." Infrared that would allow the person to track their every movement inside the house.

She passed her phone to him right as the third shot came,

and while Ruston listened for any sounds of the person trying to break in, he also studied the various frames from
the camera.

And he saw something he definitely didn't like.

"There are two of them," he relayed to her. "No infrared
device that I can see, but one is shooting at the windows in
your living room, and the other is on the front porch. How
hard will it be for him to get through the door?"

Gracelyn's groan was soft but heavy with fear. "Not hard
enough," she answered. "It's reinforced, but if he shoots
the locks..."

She didn't finish that. No need. It told Ruston everything
he needed to know. He debated making a stand since there
were only two of them, and if one of them came through
the door, Ruston would be able to take the guy out before
he managed to get inside. But it was a huge risk. If the intruder managed to get off even a single shot, it could hit
Gracelyn or the baby.

And that meant they had to move now.

Ruston took the bag from her shoulder and shifted it to
his so Gracelyn wouldn't have anything to slow her down.
He also pictured the location of the interior door that led to
the garage. It was just on the other side of the fridge. Not
ideal, since there was a window over the kitchen sink and
because the second attacker could be at the back door in a
matter of seconds.

Still, there weren't a lot of options here, and having the
baby in a bullet-resistant vehicle was better than staying
in the house that was currently under attack from two directions.

"Stay low and close to me," he instructed, though he
knew it wasn't necessary to tell her that.

Gracelyn had been a damn good cop, and she knew

how to stay alive. He hoped their combined skills would be enough to keep her infant niece safe.

They moved fast. Well, as fast as they could, considering they were crouching, and they'd just made it to the kitchen when the front doorknob rattled. Of course, it was locked. And as expected, the intruder was having none of that.

The next shot blasted into the lock.

And sent Abigail wailing.

The baby was clearly startled. And terrified. Ruston wanted to punch the intruder for doing that, for putting an innocent baby through this nightmarish ordeal.

Despite the baby's cries, Gracelyn and he kept moving. It seemed to take an eternity to go the twelve feet or so from the hall and into the kitchen, but they finally made it.

Only to hear another shot to the front lock.

And worse, someone jiggling the knob of the back door.

Clearly, these two thugs were going for a coordinated double attack. An attack where they no doubt would try to sandwich Gracelyn and him in, either to try to gun them down or force them to surrender.

Ruston felt a fresh surge of adrenaline. It was mixed with a fresh round of terror, but everything inside him managed to stay still. He relied on his training. On his instincts. And he shifted places with Gracelyn and the baby when they reached the garage door.

He hated sending her out to the garage ahead of him, but again, they didn't have a lot of options here. His shooting hand was free, and he needed to be able to return fire if those two thugs broke through the doors. Also, thankfully, there'd been no indications that someone had managed to sneak into the garage.

Gracelyn had to shift the crying baby in her arms, but the moment she opened the door, she moved into the garage. Ruston stayed put to give Gracelyn a chance to get the baby in the car seat. Once she'd finished that, he would hurry to the SUV as well.

There was a third shot to the front door, followed by what Ruston was certain was a kick and a swooshing sound. Then a single footstep. The intruder was inside.

Ruston glanced over his shoulder to see that Gracelyn was in the back seat of a black SUV and was struggling to get the baby into the infant seat. He couldn't wait any longer. He levered himself up from his crouch just enough to fire a shot in the direction of the front door. When he pulled the trigger, he heard exactly what he wanted.

Some cursing, and the sound of the guy staggering back.

Maybe he was hit, maybe he was merely scrambling to get out of the line of fire. Either way, this should give Gracelyn and him some extra seconds to escape.

Ruston aimed another shot in the direction of the back door, hoping it'd do the same to the intruder who was trying to get in there. But he didn't wait around to see or hear the results of his two shots. He bolted into the garage, hurrying to get behind the wheel.

"Stay in the back seat with the baby," Ruston told Gracelyn.

Since the keys were in the holder below the dash, Ruston was able to use the automatic starter to fire up the engine. In the same motion, he hit the remote on the visor to open the garage door.

"Stay down," he repeated to Gracelyn.

He caught only a glimpse of her face before she did just that. There was no argument in her expression, only the fear. Something he'd rarely seen in her when she'd been a cop. But this time the fear wasn't for herself or him but rather for the baby.

As soon as Ruston had enough clearance, he put the SUV into Reverse and gunned the engine. He truly hoped the thugs weren't parked nearby. Because if they had to run to their vehicles, that upped Ruston's chances of getting Gracelyn and the baby out of there.

Ruston made it out of the garage, but as he was shifting into Drive, a bullet slammed into the windshield of the SUV. It'd come from the gunman on the front porch, who was obviously very much alive. So was his partner, because Ruston caught a glimpse of the second one hurrying around the side of the house. Like his comrade, this one lifted his gun and took aim.

Two shots tore from their weapons.

Both hit the body of the SUV, causing Ruston's heart to drop. He prayed the bullets hadn't gotten through to Gracelyn and the baby. Still, he couldn't risk checking to see if they were all right. He just slammed his foot on the accelerator and got them the hell out of there.

The gunmen came after them.

Not in vehicles. Ruston didn't see any nearby. But the two men ran after the SUV with both guns blasting out nonstop shots. Most of the bullets slammed into the back window, and Ruston glanced to make sure the safety glass had held. Thankfully, it had.

He also managed to catch a glimpse of Gracelyn.

She'd gotten the crying baby in the infant seat and had positioned her body over the child. A human shield. Of course, that put Gracelyn at greater risk, but he couldn't fault her for it. If their positions had been reversed, he would have done the same.

Ruston sped to the end of the driveway, and with the tires squealing in protest, he turned right onto the narrow country road. Behind them, the shots finally stopped, but

Ruston figured that wasn't great news. It likely just meant the gunmen were running to their vehicle and would come in pursuit.

Even at the too-fast speed he was going, he was still ten minutes away from the nearest town, which happened to be Saddle Ridge. No way would backup reach them before that, even though Ruston would have loved to have a dozen police cruisers around right now. Not only would it prevent these gunmen from attacking them again, but backup would mean the thugs stood a chance of being apprehended.

And then Ruston could figure out who had hired them.

That was for later, though. For now, he focused on getting Gracelyn and the baby to safety. That started with contacting someone, and he was pleased to see that the SUV Bluetooth paired quickly with his cell so he could make a hands-free call.

He ruled out calling his sister Deputy Joelle McCullough, because she was seven months pregnant. Instead, Ruston called his brother, Slater, who was also a deputy in the Saddle Ridge Sheriff's Office. Ruston said a short prayer of relief when his brother answered on the first ring.

"Long story short," Ruston immediately said. "Get anyone you can out to the old Henderson Road. Have them head east. I want lights flashing and sirens blaring."

Slater had been a cop for a long time, and that was maybe why he didn't fire off any questions as to why Ruston would need such things. Within a couple of seconds, Ruston heard his brother make a call to Dispatch to request immediate backup and followed that by relaying the location that Ruston had given him.

"I'm on my way," Slater assured Ruston. "How far out are you from town?"

"Too far. Nine minutes." Which was an eternity. "Someone's trying to kill Gracelyn and me, and we have a baby with us."

No need for him to explain who Gracelyn was, because when Gracelyn had been his partner, he'd brought her to their family ranch several times.

"A baby," Slater muttered, and he added some ripe profanity to that. "Is anyone hurt? Do you need an ambulance?"

"No, not hurt." Ruston needed to keep it that way. "Two armed men attacked us at Gracelyn's place and will shortly be in pursuit of us again."

Ruston had barely gotten out the words when he glanced in the side mirror and saw the headlights of the vehicle barreling toward them.

"Correction," Ruston said. "The gunmen are in pursuit *now*."

That had Gracelyn shifting her position. She was still sheltering the baby, but she moved so she'd be able to use her gun.

"If they shoot out the safety glass, I'll return fire to try to get them to back off," she explained.

Ruston didn't like that plan at all, but if the bulletproof glass didn't hold, then the gunfire could get through to the baby. Having someone like Gracelyn—who was a darn good shot—returning fire could maybe get them to back off. And if she got lucky enough, she'd be able to take out the driver.

"You want to stay on the phone with me while I'm en route to you?" Slater asked him.

Ruston didn't want the distraction. He also didn't add for his brother to get there fast, because he knew Slater would. "No," he answered, and he ended the call so he could focus on the road.

Since Ruston didn't want to risk wrecking the car, he couldn't try to return fire as well, but he could do something to prevent these thugs from pulling up on the driver's side of the SUV and having an easier shot. He maneuvered into the center of the road. He should be able to see the headlights of any vehicle coming toward them and get out of the way in time.

He hoped.

Ruston kept up the pressure on the accelerator, but the gunmen must have had a more powerful engine in the big silver truck they were using, because they not only kept up, but they also gained ground. Their headlights were getting closer and closer. Worse, Ruston saw one of the thugs lean out from the passenger's window.

And take aim at the SUV.

"They're about to shoot at us," Ruston relayed to Gracelyn, hoping that would cause her to get back down.

His warning came a split second before the shot blasted into the rear window. The bulk of the glass continued to hold, but this bullet had created a fist-sized hole. It didn't seem nearly big enough for Gracelyn to get off a shot, but that didn't stop her.

She took aim. And fired. Not once. But four times.

The sound of each shot ripped through the SUV, causing the baby to wail again, but Ruston saw something positive. The truck swerved, the headlights slashing through the darkness. Gracelyn fired again. And again. Emptying the magazine.

She must have hit the driver, because the truck didn't just swerve this time. It practically flew off the road and crashed into a pasture fence.

Ruston felt some of the tightness ease up in his chest. Part of him wanted to go back and confront these SOBs, to make them pay for endangering Gracelyn and the baby. But he couldn't risk that. He just kept on driving and was about to use the hands-free system to call Slater to let him know what was going on. However, before he could do that, his phone rang.

"It's Charla," Ruston muttered when he saw the cop's name pop up on the dash screen.

"Don't tell her where we are," Gracelyn was quick to say.

She was still keeping watch out the hole in the back window but was also trying to soothe the baby. The soothing was working or else Abigail had just exhausted herself from crying, because her wails were now just a soft whimper.

"Don't tell Charla where we are," Gracelyn repeated, this time with even more emphasis.

Ruston wanted to bristle at the notion of not trusting a fellow cop. But Gracelyn was right. Someone had set him up, and only a handful of people could have managed that.

Charla was one of them.

Even though the woman had never given him a single reason not to trust her, Ruston was going to err on the side of caution here.

"What happened?" Charla demanded the moment Ruston answered the call.

Since that question could encompass a whole lot of things, Ruston took the safe route with this as well. "My cover was blown. Again. Any idea how that happened?"

There was silence for a long time, and then Charla cursed. "Blown? How? Are you hurt?"

Ruston didn't answer any of those questions but instead went with two of his own. "Why did you ask what'd happened? Why did you suspect something was wrong?"

That brought on more muttered profanity from Charla. "Because I've got a dead body on my hands. And judging from the crime scene, someone's trying to set you up for the murder."

Chapter Four

Gracelyn's heartbeat was still pounding in her ears, but she had no trouble hearing what Charla had just said.

Dead body.

Gracelyn had to choke back a sob because her mind instantly jumped to whose body that might be. Her sister's.

Sweet heaven, had Allie been murdered?

That was her first thought. Because if someone had come after Allie's baby and her, then they might have gone after Allie as well. Gracelyn needed to know the answer, but she wasn't sure she could handle it right now. Not coming on the heels of this attack that could have killed Ruston, Abigail and her.

"Who's dead?" Ruston asked.

Since Gracelyn didn't want Charla to know she was in the vehicle with Ruston, she stayed quiet. Waiting and praying.

"Marty Bennett," Charla provided. "He was found dead at his house in San Antonio. A single gunshot wound to the head."

Gracelyn felt the relief wash over her, but it didn't last. Yes, she was so thankful it hadn't been Allie, but Marty Bennett was the man who'd hired Ruston to kidnap Abigail and her.

Why was he dead?

Since he was a criminal, there could be plenty of reasons for his murder, but Gracelyn figured the man's death wasn't a coincidence. It had to be connected to this attack by those two thugs in the truck.

"Are you there, Ruston?" Charla asked.

"Yeah," he confirmed, and Gracelyn saw that, like her, he was still keeping watch around them while he drove. "I didn't kill him. Why do you think someone's trying to make it look as if I did?"

"Because whoever did kill him left your badge at the scene," Charla was quick to reply.

Ruston cursed under his breath. "My actual badge or a fake?"

"Looks like the real deal to me. Where did you last see it?"

He muttered yet more profanity. "In my apartment in San Antonio. Not the one I rent under my current cover, but my actual apartment under my real name. It's nowhere near the one I use for cover, and there are only a handful of people who know about it."

Gracelyn wondered if one of those people was Charla. Or any other cops. If not, it still meant the person behind this knew way too much about Ruston.

"I have a decent security system at the apartment," Ruston went on, "and I didn't get an alert that it'd been triggered."

"Do you have security cams?" Charla asked.

"No, but there are some on the street in front and back of the building."

"They'll be checked," Charla assured him. "I'll send someone over there now."

"No," Ruston said firmly. "Hold off on that. Uh, I'm not sure who to trust on this. With my cover blown, there could be some kind of leak."

Gracelyn hoped that his distrust extended to Charla. And maybe it did. Her distrust for Charla was certainly there. But it was possible Ruston was simply being cautious. There were plenty of reasons for that.

Maybe Ruston wanted to send up someone he'd be sure wouldn't plant anything or take something else. Then again, since the break-in had already happened, Gracelyn was betting any planting or taking had already happened.

"Where are you, Ruston?" Charla pressed a moment later.

"I'll get back to you on that," he said and ended the call.

Charla must not have cared for that abrupt dismissal, because she immediately tried to call him back, but Ruston declined it.

He looked in the rearview mirror to meet Gracelyn's gaze. "I don't know what's going on," Ruston said before he turned his attention back to their surroundings. "Do you?"

"No." And she wished her head would clear enough so she could think straight. Everything was still racing inside her, and it was hard to sort through the details when she wasn't even sure they were safe.

"Marty hired you to come after Abigail and me," Gracelyn spelled out, hoping that just going through the obvious would help them piece this together. "Then someone murdered him and tried to set you up. That someone killed Marty about the same time two gunmen were trying to kill us."

Saying it aloud worked. Something flashed in her mind. It must have come through in Ruston's, too, because he voiced what she was thinking.

"If the gunmen had killed me, then there's no way Marty's murder could have been pinned on me," he reasoned. "I spoke to Marty on the phone just minutes before the attack, which means it was probably minutes before he was murdered. I was at least fifty miles from Marty. So, the badge wasn't to set me up."

Gracelyn made a sound of agreement. "Maybe it was left to taunt you? To blow any future cover you might have?" If so, it would take Ruston off the market, so to speak. Since his face would be recognizable, he wouldn't be able to go back undercover.

Why would someone want that?

Again, Ruston supplied the answer. "This could have been done to discredit me with both the cops and the criminals." He stopped, shook his head. "And it just might work."

Yes, it possibly would, because even if Ruston had an alibi for Marty's murder, there'd still have to be an investigation. Gracelyn was betting that Ruston would be doing his own investigation, too. She certainly would be as well, since she didn't want another of these attacks.

"Either Charla or Tony could be dirty," she told him. "Of course, that's true about some other cops, but those two were in on every detail of our last assignment. And they were almost certainly in on every detail of your dealings with Marty. I've been digging into their backgrounds, and I believe there are some possible red flags for both Charla and Tony."

Thanks to the rearview mirror, she saw the concern flash in Ruston's eyes. Gracelyn didn't get to say any more, though, since there was the howl of sirens, and just ahead lights slashed across the dark road. Not solo ones either. There were at least three cruisers. In the same instant Gracelyn spotted them, Ruston's phone rang again, and this time it was Slater's name on the screen.

"Is that you coming my way in the black SUV?" Slater asked the moment Ruston answered.

"It is," Ruston verified. "We're not injured, but the SUV

is shot up courtesy of two gunmen in a silver truck. They went off the road about four miles back. It's possible one of them is injured, but they're dangerous, Slater. And they need to be caught so we can find out why they did this."

"Understood," Slater said. "Woodrow's right behind me, and the two of us will go after the gunmen. Carmen's in the third cruiser, and I'll alert her to turn around and shadow you."

Gracelyn didn't know who Woodrow and Carmen were, but she was guessing they were deputies. She was also guessing they'd come in separate cruisers to create that "lights flashing and sirens blaring" effect that Ruston had wanted. He'd gotten it, and it might be enough to put off any attackers who were nearby and ready to strike. Hopefully, though, those attackers didn't have a way to escape since they'd crashed their truck.

"Are you going to your place or the ranch?" Slater asked a second later.

"The ranch," Ruston verified, and he ended the call just as Slater and one of the other cruisers went past them.

Slater slowed just a little, probably so he could make brief eye contact with his brother and see for himself that Ruston wasn't hurt. Apparently satisfied with what he saw, Slater went off in pursuit of those gunmen with the second cruiser right behind him. The deputy in the third cruiser waited until Ruston had passed before she executed a U-turn so she could follow them.

"To the ranch?" Gracelyn questioned.

Ruston did another glance in the rearview, and he no doubt saw the concern on her face. And she didn't have to spell out why that concern was there. His father had been gunned down on the family ranch seven months ago, and

Gracelyn didn't want to jump out of the frying pan and into the fire.

"We've upgraded security since my father was killed," Ruston said.

Good, because she didn't want a killer to come waltzing in and try to finish what those two gunmen had started. Then again, she'd done plenty of security upgrades and look what'd happened. Still, there had to be a way to keep out a killer, and for Abigail's safety, she had to find it.

Had to.

Abigail wasn't her biological child, but Gracelyn couldn't have possibly loved her more. Of course, when and if Allie returned, her sister might take the baby. Or rather she would try, but Gracelyn couldn't let her do that unless she was certain the little girl was safe. At the moment, she wasn't.

Then again, maybe Allie wasn't either.

Gracelyn quickly had to shove that thought aside. No way could she let that fear take over her thoughts. She needed a clear head to keep watch. Because even though Ruston and she now had backup, they weren't out of the woods just yet.

"Red flags?" Ruston asked.

It took Gracelyn a moment to realize why he'd said that. Before Slater and the other deputies had arrived, she'd been telling him, or rather warning him, about her concerns about both Charla and Tony.

"Possible red flags," she emphasized. "It could be nothing, but I don't want to dismiss them and then have them turn out to be something." She paused a moment to gather her breath. "After our covers were blown, I did some research and found out that Charla's mother was a junkie and had a record for prostitution. When Charla was eight, her mother sold Charla's infant half brother to what was essentially a baby broker. Her mom did it again two years later with a baby girl but was caught and arrested. That's when Charla ended up in foster care."

She paused again to give Ruston a moment to digest that. It definitely fell into the "possible" red flag category, since it wasn't a strong connection to the baby farm that had come into existence some thirty years later.

"Is her mother still alive?" Ruston wanted to know.

"No. She died two years ago."

Which would have maybe been about the time of the start of the baby farm that Ruston and she had ended up investigating. Her mother's death could have been a trigger to start her on a very bad path.

Gracelyn went ahead and added the rest. "And, no, I don't have any proof that Charla stayed in touch with her mother and that the woman passed along her contacts for baby brokers to Charla. Even if she had, I know that doesn't mean Charla used those contacts to become the Green Eagle and start her own business."

Ruston muttered an agreement. What he didn't do was dismiss the possibility that it was exactly what'd happened. "And Tony? What do you have on him?"

"He was in serious debt. Not enough to draw the attention of Internal Affairs, but he'd gotten burned in a divorce settlement and was barely keeping his head above water. Until two and a half years ago, when his debts disappeared. The money appears to have come from an old army buddy of his who passed away, but I think the inheritance paperwork could be bogus."

Ruston met her gaze again. "You hacked into Tony's financials?"

Gracelyn knew she was about to admit to a crime. A crime that Ruston could use to have her arrested. But she wanted him to have the full picture here. And that picture was anything she'd learned about Tony's funds couldn't be used to launch an investigation.

"I didn't personally do the hacking," she admitted. "I don't have that particular skill set, but I hired someone to do it. An old friend of Allie's, Simon Milbrath, did it. I didn't use my real name when I contacted him. I set up an identity that I used just for my contact with him, and I never met with Simon in person."

Ruston muttered more profanity and took the turnoff to the main road. A road she knew would lead to his family's ranch.

"Simon Milbrath," he repeated as if committing that name to memory. "And Charla?" he pressed. "How did you find the info on her?"

"Not with any hacking," Gracelyn said right off the bat. "I dug through her background and found old newspaper articles about her mother's arrest. Then, using a cover that I was a reporter doing a story, I emailed the now-retired officer who arrested her mother. He was able to tell me that he had suspicions that Charla's mom had helped some of her junkie friends sell their babies through this broker. He also recalled Charla being furious when her mom was taken away."

"Did this retired cop have any computer expertise?" he asked after a short pause. "I'm just trying to get an idea of who could have found your location and then passed it along to Marty, who in turn gave it to me."

Gracelyn wanted to know the same thing, but she didn't have to consider his question for long. "I did a thorough check on the retired cop, Archie Ingram, before I ever contacted him. He's in his late seventies, and there's nothing in his background to indicate he's a computer whiz or that he was dirty. Just the opposite. He had a stellar record..."

Her words trailed off when the ranch came into view. She'd been here two other times when Ruston and she had still been partners, and it'd had a picture-postcard feel to it then, with its acres of pastures and the pretty pale yellow Victorian house. In the milky moonlight, it was still pretty, but she immediately spotted sensors on the fences, and the driveway along with the front and sides of the house had perimeter lighting. She was betting the back did, too.

"Who lives here now?" she asked. As he drove, even more lights flared on, obviously triggered by motion.

"My sister Joelle and her husband, Sheriff Duncan Holder."

She knew that Joelle was a deputy, so there'd be three cops. Maybe four if Carmen stayed. In some ways, even that didn't feel like enough protection. In other ways, it felt like too much, since Gracelyn figured she would be plenty uncomfortable around, well, anyone. That included Ruston's family.

"Do Joelle and the sheriff know we could be bringing danger right to their doorstep?" Gracelyn asked.

"They know. Slater would have told them."

She saw the tall man in the front window. Saw that he was armed, too. Duncan, no doubt, and Gracelyn recalled meeting him as well on one of her trips to Saddle Ridge. He'd been a deputy then and had obviously become the sheriff after Ruston's father had been murdered.

"A couple of months ago, there was trouble here," Ruston went on, stopping in front of the house. "Trouble at Duncan's and Joelle's houses, too. After it was over, they decided to move here and beef up security. Joelle's seven months pregnant, and they wanted to take precautions." He turned in the seat and looked at her. "They'll help us take precautions for Abigail, too."

She nodded and hoped any and all precautions would be enough. "Thank you. And thank you for helping Abigail and me to get away from those gunmen."

The corner of his mouth lifted just a little. "I suspect you could have gotten away from them yourself." The almost smile vanished. "Now, I need to figure out if I led those men to you or if they were already lying in wait to take both of us."

Yes, that was the million-dollar question, all right, but either way, the danger was still there. It could return. And despite what Ruston had just said, she wasn't so sure at all that she could have gotten away by herself.

The only reason she'd been able to return fire and cause the gunmen's truck to crash was because Ruston had been driving. If she'd been alone with Abigail and behind the wheel, it was entirely possible those thugs would have managed to overtake her and force her off the road.

When Ruston stepped out of the SUV, Duncan came out of the house, providing cover. Ruston moved fast, throwing open the back door so he could help her get Abigail unstrapped from the infant seat. The moment they'd done that, Ruston scooped up the baby. Gracelyn grabbed her go bag, and scrambling out right behind him, she hurriedly followed him into the house.

Once they were all inside, Duncan closed and locked the door. He used his phone to rearm the security system and then to make a quick call to Carmen to tell her to assist Slater. As much as Gracelyn wanted the extra backup here, it was best for Slater to have more help. That way, there was a better chance that the two gunmen would be caught.

Joelle was there in the foyer, and she was also armed.

Despite being mega-pregnant, Ruston's sister still looked more than capable of defending her family home.

"Gracelyn," Joelle said and didn't add the customary *it's good to see you*. Still, the woman didn't look upset or angry at the intrusion. Just the opposite. Joelle's face turned a little dreamy when her attention landed on the baby.

Dreamy and then suspicious. She aimed her suspicion at her brother.

"She's not our child," Ruston was quick to explain. "This is Abigail, and she's Gracelyn's niece."

Joelle seemed a little disappointed about that, and then her expression morphed again. She became all cop. "Slater said someone fired shots at you?"

Since the question seemed to be directed at Gracelyn, she nodded and hooked her go bag over her shoulder. "Two armed men. Slater and Woodrow and now Carmen are looking for them."

"I'll fill you in on the attack," Ruston added, aiming glances at both his sister and Duncan. "Any reports from Slater yet?"

Duncan shook his head. "But I've sent them out some more backup, and I've got a half dozen ranch hands patrolling the grounds."

Gracelyn was once again thankful for all these measures, but she wouldn't breathe easier until the two men were caught. Caught and questioned. Hopefully, they'd make some confessions, too.

"Any chance the baby's parents are responsible for the attack?" Duncan asked, aiming the question at Gracelyn.

She wanted to be able to say no, to deny that Allie could have had any part in this. But she couldn't. "I don't know where my sister is," Gracelyn admitted. "And Allie has a bad history with Abigail's father, Devin Blackburn."

Duncan jumped right on that. "Bad? How?"

"An arrest for assault and another for computer hacking. He also has several restraining orders from previous relationships. No jail time, though. When Allie disappeared a few weeks ago, she left me a note saying she was going back to Devin."

"Did she?" Duncan pressed.

"I'm not sure. I've been monitoring Devin's social media accounts, and there's no mention of Allie." That didn't mean, though, that Allie wasn't with him.

"Devin was also interviewed during the baby-farm investigation," Ruston supplied. "Interviewed after Gracelyn and I were attacked there," he clarified. "There was no evidence to charge him with anything."

"But you think he could be guilty," Duncan stated.

"I want to go back through the report of the interview, but Devin has the right skill set to have been involved. Computer hacker, money to set up an operation like that and a connection to a known baby broker."

Duncan nodded. "I'd like to read that report, too."

"I've gone through it many times," Gracelyn admitted. "Especially after my sister got involved with Devin."

"Was that involvement before or after the baby-farm investigation began?" Ruston asked.

"During," Gracelyn answered. "I pressed Allie about the timing, and she said she'd known Devin for years before they became lovers, and that their involvement had nothing to do with the farm. Or what happened to Ruston and me." She paused. "I don't know what's true and what's not."

But she needed to find that out fast.

Abigail whimpered, her arms flinging up in the air as if startled. Maybe from a nightmare. If so, Gracelyn hoped it was a nightmare the baby would soon forget. Still, she went to her and eased her out of Ruston's arms and into her own so she could try to soothe her.

"The nursery is already set up," Joelle explained, "so you can use that, or there's a playpen that I've already put in the guest room if you don't want to be away from her."

Gracelyn didn't even have to think about this. "The playpen." It was basically a portable enclosure that could also be used for sleeping. And it would keep Abigail with her.

Joelle nodded. "It's there and already set up. I can also have whatever you need delivered."

"Thank you, but I have some formula and diapers in my bag and there's more in the SUV." Well, unless that stash had been damaged in the gunfire. Even if it had, though, there was enough in the go bag to last for at least a couple of days.

Enough cash, too, along with a fake ID, a gun and a change of clothes for Gracelyn as well.

"Good," Joelle muttered. "But if you think of anything else, just let me know. Do you want to take her to the guest room now?"

Guest room. Not plural. And it made Gracelyn wonder if Ruston and she would be sharing it. Part of her hoped they would be. It wouldn't be especially comfortable to be in such close quarters with a man who'd once been her lover.

A onetime lover, anyway.

No, not very comfortable, but the discomfort would turn to something much worse—fear—if there wasn't enough protection for Abigail.

"I'll go ahead and take Gracelyn and the baby upstairs," Ruston offered. "Once they're settled, I'll help in any way I can with the investigation."

"I'll help, too," Gracelyn said. "I can get Abigail in the playpen and then make phone calls or anything else you

need. I don't want her out of my sight, but I need to do something to help. And please don't say I should get some rest.
That's not happening tonight, not after what we've been
through."

No one disputed that. In fact, there were sounds of agreement all the way around, and one of those sounds was from
Ruston as he led her up the stairs. The guest room was large
and just off the right of the landing, and even though the
playpen was indeed there, the lights were off. Gracelyn
kept them that way. No reason to alert anyone outside that
someone was in the room.

"I need to make a call," Ruston said, stepping to the side
of the room while she put Abigail in the playpen. "I have
to talk to a cop friend."

That gave her a shot of instant alarm, and it must have
shown on her face.

"A cop I can trust," he added, already taking out his
phone and pressing a contact number. "Noah Ryland."

She immediately relaxed. She'd worked with Detective
Noah Ryland at SAPD and believed he was trustworthy.
Since Noah was assigned to Homicide, Gracelyn figured
that was why Ruston had chosen to call him.

"Noah," Ruston greeted once the detective answered. "I
need two favors, and both are huge. I want you to secure
any and all files from Marty Bennett's residence and office.
He was murdered earlier tonight, and I don't want anything
to go missing before it's had a chance to be examined."

She couldn't hear Noah's response to that, but after a few
moments, Ruston added, "Yeah, Marty was connected to
my current undercover." Another pause. "You heard right.
Someone tried to kill me and also planted my badge at the
scene of Marty's murder."

More silence, and since she couldn't even hear any immediate murmurings from the other end of the line, she figured Noah was sorting through that info.

"Good," Ruston said after Noah finally spoke. "The second favor involves Gracelyn Wallace…Yes, the former cop…No, she didn't have a part in Marty's murder either," Ruston explained when Noah must have asked about it. "She has a solid alibi. In fact, she was with me at the time of the murder."

He paused when Noah commented on that. "Yes, with me. And that leads me to my next favor. I want to try to stop anyone from going after her again, and I need answers. Gracelyn had contact with a computer hacker named Simon Milbrath and a retired cop, Archie Ingram. It's possible one of them leaked information to Marty or someone who ended up killing Marty. So, I'd like to know if there are any known connections between Marty and them. It's possible there'll be something at Marty's residence to verify those connections if they exist."

Again, she heard Noah murmur something that had Ruston's tight jaw relaxing a bit.

"I owe you," Ruston told the detective. He thanked him, ended the call and turned to her as he put his phone away. "Noah will secure Marty's things…if they haven't already been compromised, that is."

The odds were they probably had been, but maybe the killer had gotten sloppy. If the crime had been premeditated, though, she doubted it. Still, sometimes killers made mistakes.

"Along with looking for any connections between Marty and the hacker and retired cop, Noah's also going to get the surveillance from any security cameras outside my apartment," Ruston explained. "He won't have to do it under the table, so to speak, since he's gotten approval from his lieutenant for me to view the footage in case I see something on it that'll help with the investigation."

"Good." She was glad the lieutenant hadn't tried to stonewall this. Technically, Homicide could have kept this close to the vest, but that wouldn't have benefited anyone.

Ruston scrubbed his hand over his face. "Maybe the surveillance footage hasn't been tampered with."

Again, that was a strong possibility, but unlike removing documents from Marty's home, or planting incriminating ones, it'd be trickier to alter or erase footage from traffic and security cameras.

A cop could do it, of course.

"If I caused all of this to happen, I'm sorry," Ruston muttered.

Even though she had no idea who was responsible, Gracelyn didn't intend to let Ruston fall on his sword for this. "You asked Noah to look at Simon Milbrath and Archie Ingram, and that means you think the leak of my location could have come from one of them. And it could have," she emphasized.

He made a sound of agreement, but the guilt stayed in his eyes. Ruston didn't get a chance, though, to continue voicing that guilt, because his phone rang.

"Slater," he relayed to her and immediately answered it.

Again, he didn't put the call on speaker, maybe because he thought it would wake the baby. But after only a few seconds, Gracelyn knew that Ruston was hearing bad news from his brother.

That churned up the adrenaline again and caused the mother lode of flashbacks to come at her. Not just of this attack tonight but of the one from nearly a year ago. She had to fight hard to push all of that away just so she could try to steel herself up for whatever Ruston had just learned.

It took some effort, lots of it, but she'd just managed to re-gather her breath when Ruston hung up and looked at her.

"Slater found the truck. The license plates are bogus, and the gunmen weren't inside," he relayed. "They were nowhere in sight. Slater and the others will keep looking for them," Ruston added when she groaned. "A CSI team is heading out to examine the truck now and take a sample of the blood drops that Slater spotted. I guess I was right about one of them being injured."

Good, because the blood could lead to a DNA match. She hoped the injury was so serious that it meant this snake couldn't come after them again.

"Slater said it appears the gunmen ran from the truck on foot," Slater went on. "They left a lot of stuff behind."

There was something in the way he said the last part that put her back on full alert. She waited, fighting for her breath again, while Ruston spelled it out.

"Slater had a cursory look of the inside of the truck and found my wallet," Ruston added to his account. "He figures it was taken the same time my badge was. The gunmen's plan was probably to kill you and then set me up for your murder."

Gracelyn tried to mentally work her way through that. Yes, that could have indeed been the thugs' plan. They could have waited out of sight, out of range of her cameras, until Ruston had arrived and was inside. Then they could have broken in and tried to make it look as if some kind of gunfight had gone on between Ruston and her.

"But why would they want to set you up for my murder?" she asked.

Ruston shook his head. "I'm not sure," he said and then paused again. "But there was also an infant seat in the truck. And baby things."

Gracelyn felt everything inside her tighten into a knot.

"They were going to kidnap Abigail." Her voice broke. "She was the target."

Ruston came closer, met her gaze, and he took hold of her hand. Probably because spelling it out like that had shaken Gracelyn to the core, and he'd no doubt seen that. His gentle grip helped steady her. More than Gracelyn wanted.

And that was why she stepped back.

She couldn't do this, not with the nightmares pressing so close to her that she could feel them. Memories of coming so close to them being killed ten and a half months ago.

Ruston didn't move back toward her, but their gazes stayed locked. At least they did until his phone rang again. "It's Noah," he muttered when he glanced at the screen. This time, he turned down the volume and put the call on speaker.

"Is something wrong?" Ruston asked the moment he answered.

"Yeah," Noah confirmed. "Something's very wrong. On the drive to Marty's, I made a call to a computer tech I trust so I could get a background check on Archie Ingram and Simon Milbrath." He paused. "They're both dead, Ruston. Someone murdered them."

Chapter Five

Ruston sat in one of the chairs in the guest room and, well, multitasked. He was watching the sleeping baby while Gracelyn showered in the adjoining bath. But he was also working on a laptop while drinking coffee and hoping for a miracle.

One miracle was that the caffeine would perform some magic and make him feel as if he'd gotten a decent night's sleep and now had a clear head. He'd slept some in this very chair, but that nowhere near qualified as anything decent, and so far, his head was nowhere near being clear.

Judging from the glimpse of Gracelyn's bleary eyes as she'd headed for the shower, she was in the same boat. No surprise about that. Like him, not only had she been dealing with the aftermath of the attack on them but also the flood of information they'd gotten since arriving at the ranch.

Three murders.

And all of them people who'd had a connection to either Gracelyn or him. People who could have ultimately given them the identity of the person responsible for this nightmare.

Someone was clearly cleaning up after themselves. Tying up loose ends. And Ruston needed to find something, *anything*, that would give them a break so he could learn who wanted them dead.

Unfortunately, scouring the steady stream of reports coming in and going over Devin's old interview wasn't giving him anything he could use. He figured Duncan was no doubt going through those same reports in his home office, along with coordinating this end of the investigation. That included the CSI search of the gunmen's truck and the search of the grounds of the rental where Gracelyn had been staying.

Detective Noah Ryland was keeping both Duncan and him updated about the active cases there: the three murders and the break-in at Ruston's apartment. Noah had also managed not only to get himself assigned as one of the detectives on the murders, but also to secure Marty's laptop since there hadn't been any actual paperwork in the dead man's office. The laptop was now in the hands of the IT specialist that Noah trusted.

So far, the updates from Duncan, Slater and Noah had been disappointing. And outright frustrating. Someone, somewhere, had to know something that would help make sense of all this, but for now, there were still a whole lot of questions and very few answers.

He hoped some of those questions were about to be answered when his phone dinged with a text. But it wasn't from Duncan, Slater or Noah. It was from Charla.

Where are you? Charla texted. Tony wants you at headquarters right away.

Ruston frowned and then mentally cursed. Eventually, he was going to have to meet with Tony, but he didn't want that to happen until he learned who was trying to kill Gracelyn and him.

Tony wants Gracelyn in as well, Charla added a few seconds later. You'll both need to give a statement about the attack last night.

I emailed Tony a statement, Ruston quickly pointed out, knowing what he'd given wouldn't be nearly enough. It had been the bare-bones details.

You know how this works, Charla insisted. You need to be interviewed in person.

Ruston had a quick comeback for that, too. The attack wasn't in SAPD's jurisdiction. Technically, that would fall under the duties of the county sheriff, but Duncan had already spoken to him, and he'd relinquished authority to Duncan. Charla almost certainly knew that.

Again, he didn't respond, and a few moments crawled by before Charla attempted to call him. So that the sound wouldn't wake up the baby, he'd put his phone on vibrate, and it rattled in his hand. Shortly after the rattling had stopped, he got the ding for a voicemail and listened to it.

"Damn it, Ruston, talk to me. This is important." In the voicemail, Charla huffed. "We got an anonymous tip that Marty was Green Eagle. We could finally be close to solving the case about the baby farm, and I know you want to be in on that. Call me," she demanded.

"Anonymous tip," he muttered, and, yeah, there was plenty of sarcasm in his voice.

If such a tip had indeed been phoned in, it had likely come from Marty's killer. Or someone connected to the murder, anyway. Then again, if Charla was behind this, the tip could be a lie, a ruse to try to tie all of this up.

Ruston's attention zoomed to the makeshift crib when the baby whimpered. Gracelyn had fed her less than thirty minutes earlier, before she'd gone in to take her shower, and the baby had fallen asleep during the burping process. That was when Ruston had gone down to the kitchen to get himself and Gracelyn some coffee.

The burping and so-called uptime, which Gracelyn had

explained was to minimize baby reflux, had just been coming to an end by the time he'd returned, and Abigail hadn't stirred when Gracelyn had placed her in the crib. However, she continued to squirm now, prompting Ruston to get up and move closer.

The baby still had her eyes closed but was smiling.

That made Ruston smile, too, even though he'd read somewhere that babies this age didn't actually sport that particular expression. It certainly looked like the real deal to him.

The bathroom door opened, and before he could even glance in that direction, Gracelyn blurted out, "What's wrong?"

"She's fine," Ruston assured her.

Or rather that was what he tried to do. It was obvious the reassurance hadn't worked one bit. Gracelyn ran to the baby, practically pushing him aside.

"She was just moving around a little and smiling," he added to his explanation. In fact, that smile was still on her tiny mouth.

Gracelyn released an audible breath of relief, and he could see she had to work to rein in whatever emotion had sent her running to the baby. Fear, no doubt, mixed with a whole boatload of worry.

"Sorry," she muttered. "Nerves on edge."

"No apology needed." He attempted more reassurance by giving her what he hoped would be a soothing look. This time, he was the one who failed when he saw the blood on her forehead. "You're bleeding."

She immediately pressed her fingers to a spot just inside her hairline. A spot he hadn't noticed the night before since her hair hadn't been swept away from her face the way it was now.

"It's just a small cut that I must have gotten when the safety glass was shot out in the SUV. It's okay," she insisted, taking out a tissue from the pocket of her jeans and pressing it to the wound. "I must have aggravated it when I was trying to brush my hair."

"Do you have any other cuts?" He immediately wanted to know.

"I think there's one other," she said, turning and lifting her hair so he could see the already scabbed spot on the back of her neck.

He wanted to curse. Wanted to beat those gunmen to a pulp. Yes, an extreme reaction to seeing two small cuts, but they were reminders that they could have easily been gunshot wounds.

She turned back to face him and muttered, "Yes." Gracelyn knew exactly how close they had come to dying.

He was about to fill her in on the three texts and voicemail he'd gotten from Charla, but she continued before he could do that.

"If their plan was to kidnap Abigail," she said, "those men took a huge risk shooting into the SUV."

They had indeed, and thinking about that had been a big contributor to Ruston's lack of sleep. "Maybe they did that because they panicked?" He threw the idea out there. That was one of his theories, anyway. "Or maybe because their orders were to eliminate you and me at all costs?"

It sickened him to think that the "cost" could have been the precious baby.

"The men had the infant seat in their truck," he reminded her. "And if the plan wasn't to take Abigail, then they could have just blown up the house or set it on fire with us inside."

She made a sound of agreement. "How long had you known my address before you showed up?"

"About five hours." He'd already given this plenty of thought as well. "So, maybe those men learned when I did. Perhaps Marty told them, or they found out through a mole or some kind of listening device. Either way, they would have had those five hours to figure out how to come after you." He paused. "Did you do your own security or hire someone else to set it up?"

"I did it," she answered, "with items I bought with cash the day I decided to disappear nearly a year ago. In fact, I've lived mainly off cash since then. Both Allie and I got a share of our parents' life insurance money after they died in a car crash. Allie blew through hers, but I saved mine and have been living off it since my resignation." She shook her head. "Those thugs didn't locate me through the security system, and that takes us back to Marty or someone connected to him."

Gracelyn seemed to settle a little. Ironic, since they were talking about the attack. But they were doing more than that. They were looking at this like cops and not intended victims.

"Did you get any calls or new reports when I was in the shower?" she asked.

"A few," he verified, "and basically all said the same thing. Everything is still being processed and looked at. Including Simon's and Archie's murders. Times of death for those two are about an hour apart, so the same person could have killed them both and then gone after Marty." He stopped and went through the mental checklist. "I also got three texts and a call from Charla."

The worry returned to her eyes. "She's demanding you come in?"

He nodded. "And you."

"Me? How did she know about...?" Gracelyn stopped.

"Duncan would have had to do a report, and she could have accessed it. Of course, she wouldn't have needed to access it if she already knew I was an intended target."

"Bingo." It still didn't sit well with him to think of a fellow cop as being responsible for this, but there were bad apples in every career field, and she might be one of them. "Charla says they got an anonymous tip, claiming that Marty was Green Eagle."

Gracelyn's eyes narrowed. "That's convenient."

"Isn't it, though?" he quickly agreed. "It works both ways in the killer's favor. If Marty was indeed Green Eagle, then he can't spill about anyone else who was involved in the baby-farm operation. If Marty wasn't Green Eagle, then someone wanted to set him up, probably with the hopes that setting him up would end any further investigation."

"That's one neat little package," Gracelyn muttered. "Too neat for my liking."

Ruston couldn't agree fast enough. "Let's see how this neat little package plays out. Charla will likely say that because Marty was Green Eagle, he wanted the baby for his still-ongoing business."

Gracelyn picked up on that scenario. "And that Marty wanted to get back at us for infiltrating the baby farm and causing him to have to move locations. Probably costing him a lot of money because of that. So, Marty hired you, somehow already knowing who you were. You and I were supposed to die, with you being set up for my murder."

He nodded. "But it's equally possible that Marty didn't actually orchestrate the attack against us. He could have been merely a middleman who had no connection to the baby farm or to us before someone used or hired him to set up yours and Abigail's kidnappings. He might not have had a clue how someone else was intending for this to play out. In the meantime, the cops will focus on Marty, and the real killer could just fade into the background."

"Or come after us again," Gracelyn muttered, her voice barely louder than a whisper. He saw the punch of emotion hit her, but then she quickly shook it off. "And that brings us back to Charla and Tony. Maybe," she amended. "And maybe they're clean. If so, that leaves Allie and Abigail's bio-father, Devin Blackburn."

Yes, because those two were the only other known players in this potentially lethal puzzle. Ruston had to ask, though he knew it was going to give Gracelyn another of those emotional jabs. "Could Allie have been in on the attack? Does she have a motive?"

"Trust me, I've been giving this a lot of thought," she muttered.

Of course she had. Gracelyn was still a cop at the core, and motherhood was an obvious connection they couldn't overlook.

"There'd be no obvious reason for Allie to kidnap the baby and kill us," Gracelyn said. "Obvious," she repeated. "If she wanted Abigail back, Allie knows how to get in touch with me. She could have called or texted the burner phone in my go bag. I check it often, and there was no contact from her."

Ruston figured Gracelyn had already thought of one possibility, so he voiced it. "What if Allie believed that you wouldn't give Abigail back to her? What if she thought, or someone convinced her, that kidnapping the baby was the only way she'd get her child back?"

Gracelyn's groan was soft, but it seemed to rumble through her entire body. "I wouldn't have just handed Abigail over to Allie. Not until I was certain she wouldn't do anything else reckless. And not as long as she was involved with a man like Devin Blackburn. So, yes, Allie might have known that, and Devin might have convinced her to go along with the kidnapping."

"And our murders?" he asked.

She shook her head. "Allie wouldn't have agreed to that. And, no, I'm not saying that because I'm her sister. I'm saying it because Allie isn't violent. She's, uh, more of a doormat. A very pliable, easily swayed one who Devin could have used to help him set up the kidnapping. Allie would have known what kind of security I was using, and there's a slim chance she might have even had an idea of where I was."

Ruston jumped right on that. "How?"

"I had notes on my tablet," she admitted, her forehead bunching up. That in turn caused her to wince a little, and she dabbed at the cut again. "Notes about possible rentals that I could use to make quick moves. My tablet is password protected, but there's a chance that Allie could have seen me typing and then accessed the notes without me knowing."

"Why would she have done that?" he pressed.

"Not specifically to find the notes," Gracelyn assured him. "But maybe to try to contact Devin. Or to check his social media posts." She stopped and sighed in frustration. "One minute Allie would be cursing Devin for the way he treated her, and the next, she'd be going on about forgiving him. Right before she left, she had convinced herself that she was responsible for him hitting her."

That was classic battered woman syndrome, and apparently the urge to forgive him and reunite had won out. Or maybe it had.

"You're sure Allie voluntarily left to go to Devin?" he asked.

Gracelyn opened her mouth and then immediately closed

it, obviously rethinking what she'd been about to say. "You're thinking he somehow lured Allie away?" She paused, then groaned again. "It's possible. That could go back to Allie using my tablet to get in touch with him. If she did, though, she didn't leave a trace of that contact. No copies of emails in the Sent folder or trash."

"Allie could have deleted them. Or Devin could have instructed her to delete them. You said he had an arrest for computer hacking, so he'd certainly know how to do something that simple."

"Yes," she muttered, and a moment later she repeated it while she was obviously working through this theory.

Because he was watching her, he saw the exact second she followed the theory to one possible conclusion. A bad one.

She nodded, swallowed hard. "Devin has a violent temper, and he could have lured Allie to him in order to punish her for leaving him. He could have already killed her."

Yeah. That was a bad possible conclusion, all right. Abusers could escalate. Hits and slaps could turn into something deadly.

"Oh, mercy," Gracelyn whispered, and the emotion took over.

Ruston went to her, pulling her into his arms, and she didn't resist. Gracelyn just let him hold her. Let herself lean on him while she dealt with the sickening realization that her sister could be dead. Unfortunately, that might not be the end of this scenario.

He gave Gracelyn a minute. Then two. And he just kept holding her. Definitely not a chore. In fact, it felt good to have her close like this. It stirred memories, of course. Of the heat. Of the one time they'd been together when a hug of comfort had turned into a kiss.

And then so much more.

Obviously, Gracelyn hadn't been able to deal with that *more* since she'd left the following day. That was the reason Ruston couldn't do what his body was urging him to do and push this contact further. He darn sure couldn't kiss her. That would risk her going on the run again, and he didn't want to lose her.

"If Allie is dead, if Devin killed her, then he might want to get Abigail," Ruston said. He was whispering now, too, because even though Abigail was way too young to understand, he didn't want her to hear any of this. "He might not want any DNA evidence to link him to Allie, and the baby would do that."

He felt Gracelyn's muscles tighten. "I could link him," she muttered.

Ruston eased back enough to meet her gaze. "And that leaves me. Until you told me about Allie and Devin, I had no idea about that connection."

She made a sound of agreement. "It's possible Devin contacted Marty to arrange the kidnapping, and Marty hired you." She stopped. "So, if Marty was indeed Green Eagle and knew your real identity, he could have used this opportunity to get rid of both of us and get payment from Devin for the baby."

Ruston was about to continue that line of thought, but his phone vibrated again, and he saw Noah's name on the screen. He showed it to Gracelyn, and he answered the call.

"Noah," he said, "I have Gracelyn here with me, and I'm putting you on speaker." That would save Ruston from repeating any info Noah was about to give them. And hopefully, that info would be useful and not simply more bad news. They'd filled their bad-news quota for a while.

"Good," Noah replied, "because I had a question for

her. Do you recall when you contacted retired sergeant Archie Ingram?"

"About two weeks ago," she quickly provided. "If you need the exact date, I can get it."

"Probably not necessary," Noah assured her, "but you should know that thirteen days ago, Archie called SAPD headquarters and asked to speak to Lieutenant Tony Franklin. Tony wasn't available, so Archie left a message, saying it was important, that some reporter was asking about the baby-farm investigation."

Gracelyn and Ruston exchanged glances, and she was probably thinking what he was. That this could indeed be important. If Tony had gotten concerned about a reporter, then he could have attempted to nip it in the bud. But for that to fit meant that Archie, or Tony, had figured out that Gracelyn was the bogus reporter.

"Did Tony call him back?" Ruston wanted to know.

"I'm not sure, but it's something you might want to ask him. He's on his way to Saddle Ridge, Ruston. I suspect he'll find his way to wherever you're staying."

Ruston wasn't sure whose groan was louder, his or Gracelyn's, but he thought he was the winner. "Any idea when he'll be here?"

"My guess is soon. I saw him hurrying out of his office about twenty minutes ago. Emphasis on *hurrying.*"

That would have been about the time Ruston had ended his call with Charla, and he wondered if Charla had said something to Tony to make him rush out to Saddle Ridge.

Probably.

Even if Tony didn't know where the family ranch was, he'd soon find out, and that could mean he'd be here in as soon as ten minutes. Too bad his other sister, Bree, wasn't home. Bree was a high-profile lawyer for the Texas Rangers and could create legal walls in a blink to stop Tony from getting near the ranch.

But Ruston immediately rethought that.

He didn't want to hide behind Bree and legal walls anyway. He'd talk to Tony, give whatever statement was necessary, all the while watching for any signs that the lieutenant could be a cold-blooded killer.

There was a knock at the door, and for a moment, Ruston thought that meeting with Tony would be even sooner than he'd thought. But it was Slater.

"It's me," Slater said, keeping his voice low, no doubt because of the baby.

"Thanks for the info," Ruston told Noah, and he ended the call before he opened the door.

His brother was indeed there and not alone. Joelle was with him, and she had a tray of breakfast items. Fruit bowls, pastries and some juice. "You're probably not hungry," she immediately said. "But I decided to bring it up anyway."

Ruston checked the time. Just past nine, so not late, but he realized he should have already gotten Gracelyn and himself something to eat since neither of them had had dinner the night before. And, yeah, they wouldn't be hungry, but they should still try to eat.

He thanked his sister, who had already set down the tray and was making her way to look at the baby. "How did she sleep?" Joelle asked.

"Pretty good," Gracelyn supplied. "She had a four-hour stretch before she woke up for a bottle. And now she's about an hour into a nap. She might nap for another three hours before I have to feed her again."

"Speaking of feeding," Slater said, handing Ruston a large canvas shopping bag. "Extra diapers and formula," he explained. "Joelle arranged to have it delivered."

"But I made a point of telling the store clerk I was having some serious nesting urges and that I wanted the items for the nursery," Joelle added. "That way, no one is blabbing about a baby being here at the ranch."

Gracelyn added her own thanks to Joelle. It was possible the ranch hands were aware that Abigail was here, but the fewer people who knew, the better.

They shifted their attention to Slater. Everything about Slater's expression conveyed that he didn't have good news.

"Did you find the gunmen?" Ruston came out and asked. He set the canvas bag in the chair where he'd slept.

"No, but we think we know who one of them is. The blood is at the lab, and that might take a while to process, but there was a single partial fingerprint on the passenger's-side door handle. The handle had been wiped down, but he must have missed this one. Probably because he was in a hurry to get out of there. Anyway, the CSIs ran the partial, and they got an immediate hit for a man named Terry Zimmer."

Ruston tested out the name by repeating it a couple of times, but it wasn't familiar. "Zimmer has a record? Is that why his prints were on file?"

Slater shook his head. "He was a cop in Austin and resigned after some complaints about excessive force. That was three years ago, and afterward he supposedly worked for a company that provides security for large parties, weddings and corporate events."

Ruston latched on to one word. *"Supposedly?"*

"He did work there, part-time," Slater confirmed, "but he quit a little over a year ago, and no one at the company has heard from or seen him since." He paused a moment. "The CSIs found something when they ran facial recognition on him."

Slater took out his phone, and Gracelyn and Ruston

stepped closer to look at the picture. It was a grainy shot but still clear enough for Ruston to realize what he was seeing. The sprawling Victorian house that had once been a small hotel. That'd been its purpose fifty years ago, anyway. But it had been converted into something else.

The baby farm.

This had been the place Gracelyn and he had infiltrated. The place where they'd nearly died.

Gracelyn had no trouble recognizing it either, it seemed, because Ruston heard her quick intake of breath. Despite the god-awful memories it held, though, she didn't back away. Neither did Ruston. That was because the house wasn't the only thing in the picture. There was a man dressed in dark camo, and he was armed. His stance suggested he was standing guard.

Slater zoomed in on the man's face. "This was a picture taken shortly before Gracelyn and you arrived there undercover. And that's Terry Zimmer."

Ruston's mind began to whirl with thoughts of what this might mean. One immediate question came to mind. Was this Green Eagle? Ruston's guess was no. The boss of an operation that made millions of dollars probably wouldn't have been doing guard duty.

"Why wasn't this match made after the attack?" Gracelyn wanted to know. "Why did it take so long to identify him in this picture?"

"Apparently, because there are hundreds of photos that were taken over a monthlong period when the San Antonio cops had the place under surveillance," Slater explained. "Or that's what the CSIs told me, anyway. Hundreds that are still in queues waiting to be processed. This picture was one of them, and it popped because it'd been scanned into the system, but that's about all that had been done with it."

Ruston knew it wasn't that unusual for evidence to take months to process. He only hoped that someone, like a dirty cop, hadn't purposely delayed the examination of this photo.

"Does Duncan know all of this?" Ruston asked.

Slater nodded. "I filled him in before I came up to tell you." He paused. "While I had the CSI on the phone, I asked for a quick background on Zimmer, and I got his employment history. As a rookie cop in Austin, he worked with your lieutenant."

"Tony knows him," Gracelyn muttered, sounding just as rocked by that tidbit as Ruston was.

Of course, just because Tony knew Zimmer, it didn't mean they'd stayed in contact with each other. Still, it was a connection that made Ruston very uneasy.

"Now that we have a name and a face," Slater went on, "we can put out an APB. The more lawmen looking for Zimmer, the sooner he'll be found." He locked gazes with Ruston. "Of course, the person who hired Zimmer could be sheltering him. Or trying to silence him."

Yeah, and either one of those wasn't good. Ruston didn't want Zimmer to disappear or die. He wanted answers, and after that, he wanted him in a cage for the rest of his miserable life.

"Text me a copy of that picture," Ruston said.

Slater did that before he continued. "The CSIs will continue to process the other prints they retrieved from the truck," Slater went on. But he stopped. All of them did. They froze.

Outside, Ruston heard something that tightened every muscle in his body.

A gunshot.

Chapter Six

The moment Gracelyn heard the sound, she hurried to the baby, scooped her up and scrambled away from the windows. Even though the drapes and blinds were closed, that wouldn't stop a bullet.

Part of her, the former-cop part, wanted to grab a gun and be ready to return fire, but the baby had to come first. She couldn't protect Abigail if she was doing what Slater and Ruston were doing. They had already drawn their weapons, and Ruston had hurried to one window while Slater had gone to the other. They both lifted a few slats of the blinds so they could look out.

Joelle pulled out a gun, too, from the back waist of her jeans, but instead of the window, she maneuvered herself in front of Gracelyn and the baby.

There was the popping sound of another gunshot. It didn't sound close, and neither bullet had slammed into the house. Maybe that meant the shots had come from a hunter or someone who was trying to scare off a wild animal. Gracelyn wanted to hang on to that hope, but after what'd happened the night before, this was most likely another attempt to come after all three of them.

It was an incredibly risky move.

The ranch had four cops and ranch hands, all armed.

Then again, these shots were likely coming from a sniper and it wasn't a close-range attack. It was possible the shooter thought he could pick off some of them before moving in to finish the job he'd started.

"Is everyone all right?" Duncan called out. Judging from the sound of his voice, he was downstairs.

"So far," Joelle answered. "Can you see the shooter?"

"No," Duncan replied quickly. "But it's not any of the hands." He paused a heartbeat. "Someone's coming."

Duncan added that last part just as there was a third round of gunfire. And just as Ruston muttered some profanity. "It's an SAPD cruiser," Ruston snarled. "Probably Tony."

Gracelyn shook her head. "He's not the one firing those shots."

"No," Ruston agreed. "It appears he's the one being shot at."

That definitely didn't tamp down any of Gracelyn's worries since the gunman could change targets at any second. But it did punch some holes in one of her theories that Tony might be behind the attacks.

She heard the sound of the vehicle then. The sharp squeal of brakes as it came to a stop.

"The cruiser isn't in front of the house," Ruston relayed, glancing back at her to make very brief eye contact. "He's stopped at the end of the driveway."

Gracelyn nearly asked if that was because the driver had been hit. The cruiser was bullet resistant, but that didn't mean shots couldn't get through. So, if this was indeed Tony, he could be hurt. Then again, it was also possible he hadn't wanted to come closer since the gunshots could endanger those inside.

The silence came, and it seemed to her that everyone was holding their breaths. Even Abigail wasn't making a sound.

Then Ruston's phone vibrated.

It barely made a sound, but it cut right through the silence. While he continued to volley glances out the window, he took out his phone. "Tony," he said, and he answered it on speaker. "Are you in the cruiser at the end of the driveway?" Ruston demanded.

"Yeah," Tony immediately verified. "Who's shooting at us?" There were hitches in his breath, and the question rushed out.

"I was about to ask you the same thing," Ruston countered. *"Us?"* he questioned. "Who's with you?"

"It's me," Charla said. So, their call was on speaker as well. "Are the shots maybe coming from one of the local lawmen or a ranch hand?"

"No." He huffed, and when he repeated it, there was plenty of frustration in his voice. "I think the shots came from the west. There are a lot of trees in that area, so check and see if you can spot a sniper."

Because Gracelyn was watching Ruston so closely, she saw when he shifted his attention in the direction of the road. "A Saddle Ridge cruiser is coming," Ruston relayed to everyone just as his phone dinged with a text. "Duncan says it's Luca. Deputy Luca Vanetti," he spelled out, no doubt to inform Charla and Tony. "And Duncan is Sheriff Holder. He's here inside the house."

"I don't see a sniper," Tony said. "In fact, the only people I see are the deputy in the cruiser and some cowboys with rifles back behind the house. You're sure they're not the ones who shot at us?"

"I'm sure," Ruston snapped, and this time there was

some anger in his voice. "I'm not a dirty cop, and I didn't set anyone up to be murdered."

Before Ruston could add anything to that, he got a text. "Duncan says one of the hands spotted someone in that area by the trees. It's probably the sniper, so the hands are going in pursuit."

That gave Gracelyn a jolt of both hope and fear. She wanted the ranch hands to catch the guy, but they weren't cops. And they weren't killers like the sniper almost certainly was. The ranch hands could be hurt. Or worse. Still, if they managed to capture him, then they might learn why these attacks were happening.

Or if this was actually an attack.

After everything that had happened, Gracelyn wasn't about to dole out any automatic trust to Charla and Tony simply because they'd been shot at. One of them could have arranged this, knowing their odds of being hurt while sitting in a cruiser were slim.

Slater got another text. "Luca will escort the two SAPD cops to the house. They'll stay downstairs," Slater added, glancing at Gracelyn, probably to try to reassure her that Charla and Tony wouldn't be a threat.

And they probably wouldn't be, in a house surrounded by lawmen. No, this wouldn't be an optimal time for them to try to tie up loose ends. If that was what one of them was actually trying to do, that was. But Gracelyn very much wanted to see their faces so she could maybe tell if they were trying to hide their guilt.

"We'll talk once Charla and you are inside," Ruston said to Tony, and he ended the call.

Gracelyn turned to Joelle. "Would you be able to stay up here with the baby?" she asked.

Joelle didn't jump to say yes. She looked at Ruston, and

he gave her a nod. Only then did Joelle ease Abigail into her arms.

"I'll stay up here with Joelle," Slater immediately volunteered, "but if things get dicey downstairs, let me know." He looked Ruston straight in the eyes. "Are those two cops killers?"

Ruston held his brother's gaze. "I don't know. They might both be clean, but I can't trust either of them until I know for certain they aren't behind this. Right now, I'm nowhere near certain."

Slater nodded. "Let me know if you need help," he repeated.

Ruston turned to Gracelyn, studying her, and she thought maybe he was looking for any sign that she, too, wanted to stay put. She didn't.

"I'm armed," she let him know. "And I want to hear what they have to say."

He didn't try to talk her out of it. Probably because he understood she needed to do this as much as he did. "We shouldn't accuse Charla or Tony of anything right now. Nothing to put them on the defensive. Agreed?"

Gracelyn huffed. She did agree, since the pair were more likely to talk if they thought they were all on the same side. "All right," she finally said. "I'll play nice if they do."

Ruston didn't challenge that either. "I'll text Duncan and let him know that, while both Charla and Tony are suspects, we don't have anything concrete on them. Not enough to treat them like criminals, anyway." He stopped. "I'll ask Duncan if he wants to go tough on them to try to get some answers. Duncan's instincts are good," he added. "If he senses trouble, he'll shut it down."

That was a lot of trust to put in Duncan's hands, but she reminded herself that if Ruston believed in the sheriff, then she should, too. Plus, there was that whole deal about this being a bad time for Charla or Tony to try to come after Ruston and her.

Ruston sent the text and then motioned for her to follow him. After she brushed a kiss on the baby's head, Gracelyn did just that.

Ruston didn't put away his gun as they started down the stairs, and Gracelyn kept her hand on her own weapon. There were some footsteps and movements in the foyer, and she heard Duncan.

Ruston and she followed the sound of his voice and those footsteps and found Duncan, their two visitors and a black-haired man she figured was Deputy Luca Vanetti. All four still had their weapons drawn, and it gave Gracelyn an immediate jolt. Her instincts were to take out her own gun, to be ready to defend herself, but she forced herself to stay calm.

Both Charla and Tony immediately turned to Ruston and her, and Gracelyn tried to interpret their expressions. They were both a little wild-eyed, perhaps cranked up on adrenaline from the attack. Of course, it could be a pretense, and Gracelyn wished she knew for sure.

Both Charla and Tony were what many people would call average and nondescript. Charla was five foot six with brown hair and brown eyes. Slim but not overly thin. Attractive but not beautiful. Tony was about five foot ten and had sandy-blond hair and a face that sported no scars and no unusual features.

Nothing about them stood out, which was an advantage in undercover work, something Charla still did. Tony, however, with his promotion to lieutenant, was a "suit" these days and didn't do fieldwork.

Gracelyn had always felt as if she, too, fit into that average and nondescript category. But not Ruston. No, he had one of those faces that people definitely noticed. Handsome. Hot. That should have been a disadvantage for him, but it hadn't been. He'd always managed to alter his looks just enough for undercover work, and sometimes, he'd even used those good looks to coax his way into places and situations.

"Gracelyn," Tony muttered as a greeting, and he shifted his attention to Ruston and said his name as well. "Are you two all right? Were there shots fired into the house?"

"The shots didn't come into the house," Ruston stated. "They all seemed to be aimed at your cruiser."

Ruston hadn't emphasized the word *seemed*, but Gracelyn thought it was a good addition to his explanation. Because if Charla or Tony had indeed orchestrated this, then maybe the shots hadn't even come near them.

"I heard you say the ranch hands spotted the sniper and were in pursuit," Charla piped in.

She, too, was still gulping in her breath and looking a little shell-shocked. But Gracelyn had had to do that a time or two herself when undercover and playing a role. Undercover cops had to be good actors, and that could be exactly what Tony or Charla were doing now.

It was Duncan who answered. "Yes, the hands are looking now," he confirmed, "but I have other deputies on the way. They'll set up roadblocks. We might get lucky if the shooter's still in the area."

Tony nodded, and he was visibly steadier when he looked at Ruston and her again. "We have a lot to talk about," he said, sounding very much like a boss now.

"If you're here to demand I come into headquarters—" Ruston started.

"I'm not," Tony interrupted. "Well, I was, but I'm sure as

hell not demanding it now. It's obviously not safe to try to get you into San Antonio. You either," he added to Gracelyn. "How's the baby? Is she safe?"

"She's with two cops," Gracelyn answered, rather than spell out that the baby was in the house. If Abigail was indeed the target, then there was no need to advertise her whereabouts. "Cops that I trust," she couldn't help but add.

Something flashed in Charla's eyes. Anger, maybe. And she looked ready to demand to know if that was some kind of dig. It was, of course. But Tony spoke before she could.

"I understand your distrust of the police after what happened on your last assignment," he said. His voice was oh so sympathetic. Perhaps too much so. "But we need to talk to you about the attack last night. Ruston emailed me a brief report, but we'll need your account, too."

Charla took up the explanation from there, turning toward Duncan. "We understand that this is your jurisdiction," she said to Duncan, "but we have three dead bodies, and that needs to be investigated."

Duncan glanced at Ruston, and Ruston nodded. That was apparently the only cue Duncan needed.

"We can do the interviews here," Duncan said, speaking boss-to-boss with Tony. He motioned for them to all take a seat. "And since the investigations overlap, it'd be a good time for you and your detective to answer some of my questions, too." That wasn't a suggestion. Duncan was in all-cop mode now.

Charla opened her mouth, and Gracelyn was betting she was about to protest, but she hushed when she met Tony's gaze. Apparently, Charla also responded to subtle cues.

"All right," she said, holstering her gun and reaching into her pocket.

That had Gracelyn reaching for her gun. And Charla noticed. Her eyes widened, then narrowed. "Really?" Charla snarled.

"Really," Gracelyn snarled right back. She didn't add more because she didn't want this to turn into a sniping contest. Not when she wanted those answers from Charla and Tony.

Charla made a show of taking her phone from her pocket and holding it up for Gracelyn to see. "I need to record this interview."

Duncan holstered his own gun, took out his phone and sat in one of the chairs. "And I'll record your responses." He clicked on the record function. "In fact, I'd like to start. Sheriff Duncan Holder conducting interview of... State your names for the record," he insisted.

Charla and Tony were clearly not pleased to be on the other end of what would likely turn out to be an interrogation, but they both gave their names and sat on the sofa across from Duncan.

Duncan stated the date and time and continued. "Someone blew Detective Ruston McCullough's cover while he was on assignment at a house in my jurisdiction, and it nearly got him and Gracelyn Wallace killed. Who did that? Who's responsible for not securing the location of an undercover officer?"

Gracelyn had to suppress a smile. She was so glad Duncan had taken over the bad-cop role, and he'd almost certainly done that on purpose so that Tony and Charla's venom would be aimed at him. Of course, some of that venom would no doubt still come at Ruston and her. And she welcomed it. Because angry people often let things slip.

"That's being investigated," Tony answered. Yes, there was ire, all right. "We're still in the preliminary stages of that, but it's my theory that no one in my department was responsible. I trust the cops who work for me."

"Including Ruston?" Duncan asked.

Tony blinked. "Of course."

"Then that means you don't believe he was responsible in any way for his cover being blown," Duncan quickly concluded.

Tony shook his head, maybe objecting to the *in any way* part, but Duncan didn't give him a chance to voice that.

"For the record, Lieutenant Franklin indicated non-verbally that he did not believe Detective Ruston McCullough compromised his undercover identity. Is that right?"

"That's right," Tony muttered.

"Good. So, if Ruston didn't tell anyone who and where he was," Duncan went on, "then who did? What's your theory?"

Charla huffed. "That the leak came from Marty Bennett, the man who hired Ruston's undercover persona."

"Marty, who's now dead," Duncan stated in a way that made it sound like "isn't that convenient" sarcasm. "And how would Marty have learned Ruston was a cop?"

"We don't know," Tony jumped in. He met Ruston's gaze. "Not yet. But we'll find out. That's why we're here. I need to know if there's any possibility that you gave Marty some information, no matter how small, that made him believe you were undercover and that this was a sting operation."

Now it was Ruston who huffed. "So, you do think I was responsible for the leak. Trust me, I wasn't. My life was on the line. Gracelyn's life and the baby's, too. No way would I have risked letting anyone know. Especially a lowlife like Marty."

Duncan sat back, and Gracelyn took that as another of

those subtle cues that he was relinquishing the interview to Ruston and her. Gracelyn went with it.

"I certainly didn't leak my location to anyone," Gracelyn stated, easing down onto the love seat that was positioned adjacent to the sofa and the chair where Duncan was seated. "And until Ruston showed up, I had no idea he was even coming. But those two gunmen who tried to kill us, they knew. They knew my exact location."

"Which they could have gotten from Marty," Charla interjected.

"And that leads us right back to the question of who told Marty," Ruston said, sitting next to Gracelyn. "It's not just Gracelyn's location either, but considering the break-in at my apartment, someone would have told either Marty or his killer about that, too. That's a lot of information for someone outside of SAPD to have."

"We're looking into that," Tony insisted, and he shifted his attention to Gracelyn. "Is it possible you alerted someone to Ruston's identity—"

"No," she interrupted, "because I didn't know his undercover identity."

"But you knew the location of his apartment," Charla quickly inferred. There was something in her tone that suggested Charla had guessed that Ruston and she had gone there because they'd been lovers.

"No," Gracelyn repeated. "I didn't."

Charla pulled back her shoulders, and it seemed as if she wanted to challenge that. "But you came here with him. Before last night, I mean. You visited Ruston here in Saddle Ridge."

Gracelyn let her smile come. "That wouldn't have been in any report, Charla. How would you know that?"

"I must have heard it somewhere," Charla muttered, but

her eyes were narrowed now. "What is this about?" she demanded. "You can't possibly think Tony and I had something to do with what happened?"

"Did you?" Ruston asked, and he used some of Tony's wording to phrase his next question. "Is there any possibility that you gave Marty information, no matter how small, that ended up blowing my cover?"

"Absolutely not," Tony insisted.

Ruston didn't miss a beat. He took out his phone, brought up the photo he'd gotten from Slater and held it out for Tony to see.

"This is one of the gunmen who tried to kill us," Ruston spelled out. "Recognize him?" His tone indicated he already knew the answer.

A muscle tightened in Tony's jaw. "Terry Zimmer. How the hell do you know he was involved?"

"Evidence gathered from the vehicle used in the attack," Duncan supplied. He checked the time. "It's been less than fifteen hours since that attack, and we—a small-town sheriff's office with limited resources—have identified a former cop who you personally not only know, but one who also tried to murder Ruston and Gracelyn. And he was connected to the baby farm. You know the one I'm talking about. Gracelyn and Ruston were nearly killed then, too."

"How do you know that?" Tony demanded, but then he waved off the question. "I haven't seen or spoken to Zimmer in over a decade."

"Good," Duncan said, and he breezed right on. "Because as we speak, I have the Texas Rangers doing a deep background check on Zimmer. Deep," he emphasized. "So, you want to rethink that answer?"

"No." Tony spoke through clenched teeth now. "And there was no reason to involve the Rangers."

"Beg to differ," Duncan argued. "I have a high-ranking cop in SAPD—that would be you—with connections to a man involved in both an illegal black-market baby operation and the two attempted murders of police officers. I don't want this swept under any rug. I want everything out in the open."

The anger came, flaring through Tony's eyes, and he whipped out his phone, his movement so fast that it had Luca, Duncan, Ruston and Gracelyn all drawing their weapons. That caused Tony to scowl.

"Since you've brought in the Rangers," Tony said, his tone icy now, "you'll want to let them know about Gracelyn's involvement in this. And, no, I don't mean the so-called attempts to kill her. I mean her involvement."

Gracelyn flashed him her own scowl, but the uneasiness fell on her like a dead weight. She didn't ask what Tony meant by that, but it was obvious he had something up his sleeve. Or rather on his phone, because he thrust it out for her to see.

She leaned in closer, looking at the image that was just as grainy as the one they had of Zimmer.

"This was taken from the security camera just up the street from Marty's house," Tony explained, keeping his steely stare on Gracelyn. "Notice the time stamp."

She did. It would have been around the time that Marty had been murdered. There was the vague image of someone dressed in dark clothes.

Tony enlarged the image and showed it to her. Gracelyn leaned in again. And saw the face. She managed to choke back a gasp. Barely. But inside, a firestorm of emotions came at her.

Because she was looking at her sister's face.

Chapter Seven

Ruston wanted to curse. Something that Gracelyn likely wanted to do as well, and like him, she was no doubt trying to absorb the shock of what they were seeing.

Allie.

Near a murder scene.

No way could Ruston convince anyone, including himself, that Allie had simply been in the wrong place at the wrong time. That would be way too much of a coincidence.

"That's your sister, right?" Tony asked.

Gracelyn nodded. "Yes, that's Allie."

Both Tony and Charla had smug looks on their faces. "And what was she doing there?" Charla demanded.

Gracelyn shook her head. "I don't know. I haven't heard from her in a while, so I didn't know where she was."

"Well, clearly she was at the house, or at least near the house, of a man who was murdered," Charla said. "So, it's highly likely that she's the one who compromised Ruston's identity."

"No," Ruston was quick to argue. "There's nothing highly likely about that scenario. I had absolutely no indication from Marty that Allie was involved with this."

Of course, Marty wouldn't have mentioned that if she had been, but the premise was still way off.

He hoped.

Because if Allie was truly involved, this was going to crush Gracelyn. However, it might not be that much of a shock once it all sank in, and Gracelyn would likely come to some conclusions.

There was one way this could have all fit.

One way to explain why Allie had been there.

Ruston, though, had no intentions of voicing it in front of Charla and Tony. Thankfully, he didn't have to, because Tony's phone rang, and he saw Captain Katelyn O'Malley's name on the screen. Tony's boss. That wiped any trace of a smirk off Tony's face, and he stood, stepping to the side and muttering something about having to take the call.

"Why was your sister there?" Charla demanded, obviously trying to continue this interview.

But Tony's call only lasted a couple of seconds, and when he turned back around, Ruston thought the lieutenant looked even more riled than when they'd been peppering him with questions.

"I have to go," Tony said, motioning for Charla to stand. He aimed those anger-filled eyes at Duncan and then Ruston. "Captain O'Malley got a call from the Texas Rangers, and they want to talk to me about my association with Zimmer. And it apparently can't wait."

Ruston could have managed his own smirk, but he didn't. He just considered this progress, because if there was something dirty going on with Tony's connection with Zimmer, maybe the Rangers could find it.

Charla clearly wasn't pleased with any of this, and she huffed. "The sniper could still be out there," she reminded Tony.

"Then we'll be careful." Tony looked at Ruston again.

"But it might not be necessary. The shots could have just been a way to try to ward us off."

Tony was obviously suggesting that Ruston and his family were behind the shooting. Of course, they weren't, but the gunfire could have indeed been a warning. The killer might want to discourage police interference if he wasn't linked to Tony or Charla.

And that brought him back to Allie.

Tony got Charla moving, and despite the intense exchange that had gone on during the interviews, Luca, Duncan and Ruston all provided cover as Tony and Charla hurried down the porch steps and to the waiting cruiser. Gracelyn drew her weapon as well, but thankfully stayed in the door.

Ruston held his breath when no shots came, and he rushed back in, mainly so he could get Gracelyn fully back inside. He expected her to still have that shell-shocked look on her face, but she had shaken that off.

"I need to try to call Allie," she insisted.

"You know how to get in touch with her?" Duncan asked, shutting the door and resetting the security system.

Gracelyn nodded, then lifted her shoulder as if not so certain of her response. "I gave her a burner before she left and told her if I needed to contact her, I'd call her with a burner I keep in my go bag. Or that I'd message her through a private Facebook page I'd set up. I'll try the phone first."

"I'll get your go bag," Duncan offered when she started for the stairs. "I want to check on Joelle anyway."

"And I need to text one of the ranch hands to see where they are in their search for the sniper," Luca explained, taking out his phone and moving away from them.

Ruston had no doubts that Duncan did want to check on Joelle and that Luca needed to make contact with the ranch hands, but he also figured this was about giving Gracelyn and him a moment alone. Gracelyn clearly needed it, because she went straight into his arms.

"Oh, God," she muttered. "I'm so sorry."

He'd expected this from her, but it still riled him. "You aren't going to take the blame for anything your sister might have done. If she did anything at all," he tacked on to that. "Someone could have lured her there to Marty's."

Gracelyn made a half-hearted sound of agreement. "But even if she had been lured, it means someone used her to get to you. To try to kill you."

"And you," he pointed out. As good as it felt to hold her, and it felt darn good, he pulled back just enough so he could look her straight in the eyes. "Play this through while thinking like a cop and not like the sister of a woman who's screwed up time and time again."

She stared at him, and he saw the shift. He saw Gracelyn tucking away some of the raw emotion that had to be eating away at her. "All right." She repeated that several times. "I don't recall Allie ever mentioning anyone named Marty, so she might not have even known him." She paused. "And she might not have been in that area because of him."

Bingo. "Where does Devin Blackburn live?" he asked.

"One of those upscale apartments on the River Walk in San Antonio. I've never been there, and he also owns a house in a gated community on the north side of the city. I've never been to it either," she was quick to add. "But after Allie told me some of the things he's done, I researched him."

"Are either of those two places anywhere near Marty's?" He pulled out his phone and showed her first the location of Marty's office and then the man's house, where he'd been murdered.

She looked at the addresses on the map, sighed and shook her head. "No."

"But maybe Allie is staying near there," he pointed out. "You don't know for certain she's with Devin."

That put some hope in her eyes. "True. Things might not have worked out between them." She paused, huffed. "Of course, that doesn't explain why Allie wouldn't have tried to come back to get Abigail."

No, it didn't. But there was something else that had to give Gracelyn hope. "Allie's alive, and she didn't appear to be hurt." He wanted to see the actual surveillance footage, though, so he could try to determine what direction she'd come from and if anyone had been with her.

Since Noah was one of the detectives investigating Marty's murder, Ruston sent him a text to request a copy of the security feed. Of course, Noah would almost certainly scour that feed for himself, looking for anything that would help him find Marty's killer.

"I swear, I won't fall apart," Gracelyn muttered.

Ruston looked down at her. They were still close. Very close with their bodies touching. "I never thought you would," he let her know.

She shook her head. "I fell apart nearly a year ago when we were almost killed."

"No." He pulled her back into his arms, creating even more contact, but hopefully giving Gracelyn something she needed right now. "You never fell apart. If you had, you wouldn't have been able to put together a plan to disappear the way you did."

Even though he could no longer see her face, Ruston suspected she was sporting a very skeptical expression. "I disappeared," she stated.

"Because you needed time to process what'd happened,"

he spelled out. "And while I would have preferred you process that with me around, I understand why you had to have that time, that space."

She lifted her head and looked up at him as he looked down at her. "Yes," she muttered. "You understand because of your father."

Yeah, he did. And Ruston was well aware that his father's life had ended just a few yards from where they were standing right now. Ruston had done his own version of disappearing in the weeks following that. He'd thrown himself into the investigation. He'd become obsessed with finding his father's killer. That obsession was still there. Maybe it always would be until his dad finally got the justice he deserved.

First, though, he had to unravel who was after Gracelyn and him. That was the only way to keep the baby and her safe.

She groaned softly, causing Ruston to look at her again. Not that his attention had strayed too far. And it didn't stray now either. With their gazes locked, things passed between them. The worry. The urgency to find their attacker.

The heat.

Yeah, it was there, all right, and it felt like a gut punch of a different kind. It was also a complication. One that he knew he shouldn't act on. But he did anyway.

Ruston dipped his head and kissed her.

Since he hadn't actually planned it, he wasn't sure if this was for comfort or if the heat was calling the shots here. When the taste of her jolted through him, he had his answer.

The heat was in charge.

That definitely wasn't a good sign, and he figured Gracelyn would realize that and push him away. She didn't. She sank right into the kiss, pressing her mouth harder against his. Deepening it, too, and skyrocketing the fire. Making every inch of him want every inch of her.

The sound of approaching footsteps had Gracelyn and him practically jumping away from each other. Not in time, though, for Duncan to miss what'd been going on. Duncan didn't question it, not verbally, but Ruston figured the look Duncan gave him was sort of a caution. *You're playing with fire.*

Ruston knew that was the truth. This heat between Gracelyn and him was strong and hot. It was also a distraction. One that could ultimately cause him to lose focus at a time when that could turn out to be a fatal mistake. Still, Ruston couldn't just flip a switch and put an end to the heat. He just needed to try to keep it in check until Gracelyn and the baby were no longer in danger.

Duncan handed Gracelyn the go bag. "Joelle says she'll stay with the baby as long as needed," he said while Gracelyn began to dig through the bag for the burner phone. "I'm hoping you'll let her do that."

Gracelyn looked up at him, and Duncan huffed. "I'm worried about her. She's a cop to the bone, but she's also pregnant. I'd rather her be with Abigail than facing down murder suspects."

Since Joelle was his sister, Ruston felt the same way. It was even more of a reason for them to find the killer and put a stop to the danger.

"With Allie on that surveillance footage, SAPD will bring her in for questioning," Ruston told Duncan. "If they can find her, that is."

"I'd like to question her, too," Duncan insisted. "And her boyfriend, Devin Blackburn."

That was exactly what Ruston had hoped he would say.

First, though, they had to locate Allie, and that started with the phone call.

"You'll probably want to record this in case Allie answers," Gracelyn said.

She waited until Ruston had hit the recording app on his phone before she used the burner to dial the only number in its contacts. Gracelyn then put it on speaker just as it rang.

And rang.

After what felt like an eternity, it went to voicemail, but there was no personal recorded greeting to invite the caller to leave a message. Just the beep.

"It's me," Gracelyn said. Ruston figured she purposely didn't leave her name in case someone other than Allie had access to the burner. "We need to talk. It's important."

She ended the call, slipped the burner into the pocket of her jeans and took out her other phone. "I'll leave a message on the private Facebook page, too," she added and did that as soon as she pulled up the app.

When Ruston heard the ringing, he at first thought it was Allie returning her sister's call, but it was his own phone.

"Noah," he relayed to Gracelyn and Duncan, and he took the call on speaker. Gracelyn stopped what she was doing and moved closer to listen.

"I just heard someone shot at Tony and Charla," Noah said right off the bat.

Ruston realized he should have added that to the text he'd sent to Noah earlier. "Yeah," he verified. "They're both okay. The sniper hasn't been found, but Tony and Charla are headed back to San Antonio."

"Glad to hear they weren't hurt. Does their departure have anything to do with the Texas Rangers being in Captain O'Malley's office?" Noah asked.

"It does." And this was yet something else he should have

told Noah about. "There was a fingerprint in our attackers' truck that belonged to former cop Terry Zimmer. He was also connected to the baby farm. And Tony. They were rookies together in Austin."

Noah said a few words of choice profanity. "Yeah, that would get him in the captain's office." He paused a second. "You really think Tony could be dirty?"

Ruston didn't want to think it, but there was no way he could deny the possibility. "Either that or someone came by a whole lot of information that shouldn't have been available to anyone but cops."

Noah made a sound of agreement. "Terry Zimmer," he repeated. "I'm plugging his name into a search engine I put together. It's sort of a cop's form of Google that taps into data pools of arrest histories, police reports and witness statements. I'll let that run while I tell you the main reason I'm calling." He paused. "There's a problem with Marty's computer files."

Now it was Ruston who cursed, and Gracelyn wasn't far behind him on that particular reaction. "What happened? Did they go missing?" Ruston asked.

"No, but they might as well have." There was plenty of frustration in Noah's voice. "The techs say it was some kind of complex computer virus that corrupted every file on the laptop. They'll see if they can get anything from the corrupted data, but it doesn't look promising."

Hell. Of course, Marty would put some kind of measure like this in place. Except Ruston rethought that. "Any chance the virus was added after the laptop was taken into custody?"

"I asked the techs about that, and they say the virus doesn't appear to have been uploaded remotely, that they think it was already on the computer."

So, the killer likely hadn't done that. If he'd gotten access to Marty's laptop, he could have just destroyed it. Unless... "Any chance those files were backed up on a storage cloud?"

"Yes," Noah verified, "and those copies were corrupted, too." He stopped, muttered something that Ruston didn't catch. "Hold on a second," Noah added. Then he cursed again. "You said Tony knows Zimmer, but you didn't mention that Charla does, too."

Ruston saw the surprise register on Gracelyn's face and figured it was on his as well. "Because I had no idea. And she didn't say a word about it."

"Well, she knows him, all right. According to a report Charla filed last year, Zimmer was her confidential informant."

Ruston went still. "Give me the details on that, please." He wanted one bit of info in particular. "Was it connected to the baby farm?"

"I'll read it thoroughly but just scanning through for now," Noah let him know. "But, no, it doesn't appear to have anything to do with the baby farm. This report was filed about a month after the attack on you and Gracelyn. Charla was undercover to investigate some illegal weapons being moved through and stored in a warehouse. The weapons were found, and Charla noted that Zimmer had provided her with info for which he was paid."

So, that might be why Zimmer had been actually named. The payment would have required an invoice.

"Anything in that report about Charla investigating Zimmer before she used his info?" Ruston asked. Because if Charla had run a deep background check, she might have found a photo of him at the baby farm.

"Nothing that I can see," Noah answered. "But like I said,

I'm skimming. I'll go through this line by line, and I'll keep running the search engines. If I find anything, I'll let you know. Oh, and you'll be getting a copy of the surveillance feed sometime today."

Ruston thanked him and ended the call just as another phone rang. The burner this time. Gracelyn yanked it from her pocket but didn't answer it on speaker until Ruston had the recording app going.

"I understand you want to talk to Allie," the man said.

"Who is this?" Gracelyn demanded.

"Devin Blackburn," he said without hesitation.

Ruston didn't like this one bit. Clearly, neither did Gracelyn. "Where's Allie? Why are you using her phone?"

Devin countered that with a question of his own. "Are you Gracelyn?"

Gracelyn hesitated but finally said, "Yes. Where's Allie?" she repeated.

Devin's sigh was loud and long. "That's what I was hoping you could tell me. I don't know where your sister is."

"But you have her phone," Gracelyn quickly pointed out.

"No, I have a phone that I found in her purse. It's not the one she usually uses. When I heard it ringing, I didn't get to it in time to answer it, but I listened to your voicemail. I figured from your tone that you're worried about her. Well, so am I. Do you have any idea where Allie is?"

The image of Allie on the security footage flashed into Ruston's head, and he was certain the same image was going through Gracelyn's.

"When is the last time you saw my sister?" Gracelyn pressed.

"Two days ago." Devin didn't hesitate, but then he sighed again. "I'm afraid Allie has gotten into serious trouble."

Some of the color drained from Gracelyn's face. "What do you mean?"

Devin wasn't so quick to answer this time. "We have to talk, and it should be in person. You can either come to me, or I can meet you somewhere."

Gracelyn paused, too. "Meet me at the Saddle Ridge Sheriff's Office."

Ruston expected Devin to balk about the location. He didn't. "Saddle Ridge Sheriff's Office," he confirmed. "I can be there in an hour. See you then."

"Wait," Gracelyn said before he could hang up. "What kind of trouble is Allie in?"

No sigh this time but rather a soft groan. "The kind that can get her killed. Let's see if we can prevent that from happening."

Chapter Eight

Gracelyn was fully aware this wasn't the safest thing to do. Meeting Devin meant leaving the ranch. Leaving Abigail. And Ruston and her going outside when there was a sniper still at large. But after talking it over with Ruston, they had decided it was a risk they had to take.

Because they needed to hear what Devin had to say.

And they didn't want to do the interview at the ranch. Better to have some distance between Abigail and him, even if that distance meant more of a risk to Ruston and her. A risk, though, that didn't compromise Abigail's safety.

That was why Ruston and she had arranged for plenty of protection, with Slater, Luca and Joelle all staying with the baby while the armed ranch hands patrolled the grounds. A sniper could still return to fire more shots, but any gunfire was more likely to be aimed at Ruston and her. That was why they were all keeping watch as Duncan drove them to the sheriff's office.

A drive that hopefully wouldn't turn out to be a huge mistake.

Gracelyn needed to know what was going on with Allie, and Devin might be able to give her answers. And if she was to believe what Devin had said, they were answers that might help save Allie's life. She wasn't close to her sister, wasn't even sure she could say she actually loved her, but Gracelyn certainly didn't want Allie hurt or dead.

What she wanted, though, was to talk to Allie. That was critical. And Gracelyn hadn't given up hope of that happening. It was the reason she'd brought the burner with her, and she'd also left a message for Allie on that private Facebook page. Since Allie didn't have the burner Gracelyn had given her—Devin did—maybe Allie would use her regular phone, see the Facebook message and get in touch with her.

Because Ruston and she were in the back seat of the cruiser, Gracelyn had turned to keep watch behind them. To make sure they weren't being followed. Ruston was watching the sides of the narrow road while Duncan focused on the driving and what was ahead. All of them were primed for an attack, and they stayed that way during the entire ten-minute drive, even though they didn't see another vehicle until they were in town.

Duncan parked, and they used the side door to enter the building to get to his office. Gracelyn had been here before, too, when Ruston's father was sheriff, and it appeared that Duncan had kept things exactly the same, down to the Texas landscape art on the walls.

His office front was all glass, so she had no trouble seeing into the large bullpen and reception area, where she immediately spotted two deputies. She was pretty sure they were Carmen Gonzales and Woodrow Leonard, and both were on the phone while Carmen was also using her computer. However, the moment she noticed Duncan, she ended the call and stood.

"Devin Blackburn's not here yet," she relayed to Duncan. "And we're still waiting on those two officers to come down and pick up the prisoner."

"What prisoner?" Ruston asked.

"A guy named Brent Litton," Duncan supplied. "Woodrow pulled him over for speeding, and when he ran the plates, it came up there was an outstanding warrant on him for a string of burglaries in Austin. Austin PD is supposed to come and get him sometime today." He looked at Gracelyn and must have seen the concern on her face. "This guy isn't the sniper. He's been behind bars since about ten last night."

Gracelyn wished he had been the sniper so they could have questioned him. Additionally, he would have no longer been a threat.

"I need you to sign some reports," Carmen continued, still speaking to Duncan.

The deputy picked up a folder and started toward him, but Duncan went to her in the bullpen. Again, Gracelyn thought he'd maybe done that to give Ruston and her a little privacy so she could settle her nerves. But there wasn't any time for that because Ruston's phone rang, and when he took it from his pocket, she saw Noah's name on the screen.

"Devin's not here yet," Ruston told Noah the moment he answered. Ruston had already filled Noah in on Devin's phone call, and Noah had to be just as anxious as they were to find out what the man had to say.

"I hope he hasn't had second thoughts," Noah muttered. "Up to now, he's been dodging my calls and requests to come in for an interview. And I don't have enough for a warrant. In fact, I don't have anything on him except his involvement with Allie."

Yes, and that was why they had to get more. Well, if there was more to get, that was. It was entirely possible that Devin had nothing to do with any of this.

"I'm about to email you the surveillance footage of Gracelyn's sister," Noah continued a moment later. "I wanted to take care of that because I think Tony's trying to have me taken off Marty's murder. He's pissed off, Ruston, and he knows we're friends."

"He also knows you're a good cop," Ruston snarled. "Is he purposely trying to compromise the investigation?"

"I hope not, but the possibility has occurred to me. I don't think he'll succeed in getting me removed," Noah added. "He's having to deal with both the Rangers and Internal Affairs. This is gossip, but word is there are some inconsistencies in his finances and that he'll be put on paid leave for a couple of days."

That definitely wouldn't make Tony happy, but Gracelyn was thankful this was being done. Because there were inconsistencies, and if they had anything to do with the murders and attacks, then that should come to light.

"What about Charla?" Gracelyn asked. "Is Internal Affairs looking at her, too?"

"Not that I know of, and she wasn't in the meeting with the captain and the Rangers." Noah paused. "Is Charla aware that the two of you know about her connection to Zimmer?"

"Not yet," Ruston answered. "I wanted to confront her with that myself to see her reaction, and then I'll pass the info along."

Normally, the passing along meant her boss would be the one who got that info, but since her boss was Tony, that would likely be elevated to the captain.

The front door opened, and a dark-haired man came in. Devin. She recognized him from his photos.

"Gotta go," Ruston told Noah. "Allie's boyfriend just showed up."

"Good. Let me know if he spills anything I can use," Noah added right before he ended the call.

Gracelyn's first impression of Devin was that he didn't look the sort to spill anything that wouldn't paint himself in a good light. But that left plenty of other areas where he might be helpful. First, though, she had to get past that initial feeling of disdain. This was a man who'd assaulted and stalked women. That made him slime in her book, but if she hadn't known his history, she might not have seen the sliminess.

He was dressed like a rock star in his designer jeans with rips in all the trendy places. He'd paired them with a black tee that she was betting he hadn't bought off the rack. Expensive boots and sunglasses completed the outfit.

Woodrow went to Devin, first checking his ID and then sending him through the metal detector. No alarms sounded, but then, Devin would have been a fool to come to a sheriff's office armed.

"Gracelyn?" Devin questioned once he'd cleared security. When she nodded, he thrust out his hand for her to shake. She did that while keeping her gaze pinned to him.

"We can use interview room one," Duncan said, and he introduced both himself and Ruston.

"We?" Devin challenged. "I thought it'd be just Gracelyn and me talking."

"Then you thought wrong," Duncan quickly replied.

Devin didn't scowl at that remark. In fact, the little twist of his mouth seemed to convey that he'd expected this to be an official interview with the cops.

"Detective Noah Ryland from SAPD has been trying to get in touch with you," Ruston said to Devin as they walked to the room.

"Really?" Devin said, and he checked his phone. "No messages from him. Oh," he added as if something had just occurred to him. "I have a new number. Guess he's probably been trying to reach me at the old one. Detective Ryland, you said?"

Ruston nodded. He, too, had a hard look in his eyes.

"All right, I'll call Ryland when I'm done here," Devin said once they were in the interview room. "I'm guessing he wants to talk to me about Allie," he added. "Has she done something else I don't know about?"

None of them answered, but Duncan launched right into reading Devin his rights. That finally erased some of Devin's cockiness.

"Am I under arrest?" Devin asked.

"No. Reading you your rights is for your protection, so that you know what's expected of you," Duncan explained. "And so you're aware you can have a lawyer. We can all wait here if you want to call one."

"That won't be necessary. I didn't do anything wrong," Devin insisted. "In fact, I'm trying to do what's right by coming here." He sat and looked at Gracelyn, who took the seat at the table across from him. Duncan sat next to her while Ruston opted to stand.

Gracelyn didn't waste any time getting the questions started. "On the phone, you said you were afraid my sister had gotten into serious trouble. Explain that."

Devin gathered his breath, and rearranged his expression by bunching up his forehead. "Allie's been using drugs again. Two days ago, I caught her trying to make a deal with one of her old dealers. She didn't even deny it. Didn't deny either that she'd taken money from my wallet to buy the drugs."

Gracelyn tried to ignore the initial emotional punch of that. It certainly wasn't the first time she'd heard someone say Allie was using. In fact, Allie had been arrested twice for drug possession when she'd been a juvenile. Her pattern was to stay clean for about a year, and then she'd have a relapse. Thankfully, she'd been in the clean stage when she was pregnant with Abigail.

"Allie and I had a big argument," Devin went on, "and I told her she had to leave. I've got a record." He added a dry laugh. "But I'm positive you already know that." He put his arms on the table and leaned in toward her. "I don't want to do anything that could land me in jail. Not only would that cause my folks to disown me, but it's not who I am now. New leaf and all that."

Gracelyn figured she failed at totally suppressing a scowl over the way he'd flippantly thrown in that last part. But she was betting he was indeed concerned about being disowned. From everything she'd read about his parents, they fit more of the mold of upstanding citizens.

"Where did Allie go after you argued?" Gracelyn asked.

"I have no idea." He paused, forehead bunching up again. "But she said if I didn't give her the money that she'd get it from you. She figured by now you were attached to the baby and that you'd be willing to pay for the privilege of keeping her."

Gracelyn felt sick to her stomach, and she wanted every word of that to be lies. But she couldn't be sure. When Allie was using, she would resort to anything to get her hands on drugs.

"So, you know about the baby," Ruston commented.

"Yeah, Allie told me about her." Devin stopped, and his eyes widened. "Wait. Is the kid okay? Is she safe?" The concern in his voice appeared to be genuine. *Appeared.*

"She's safe," Gracelyn settled on saying. "What did Allie tell you about the baby?"

"That I'm her father," Devin admitted without hesitation.

"Are you?" Gracelyn pressed, though she thought she

already knew the answer. It was the eyes. Abigail's eyes were a genetic copy of Devin's.

Devin shrugged. "It's a good possibility that I am. I mean, the timing fits. Allie and I had been together for a while before she left. Another argument," he tacked on to that.

"Yes, I remember seeing the bruises and her black eye," Gracelyn remarked. She sounded as if she had ice in her blood, but it was all fiery anger.

Devin held up his hands. "She didn't get those from me. Scout's honor." He made a crossing gesture over his heart. "She got those from her dealer."

"She wasn't using when I saw her with the bruises," Gracelyn argued, and this time the anger coated her words.

"No," Devin agreed, "but she'd agreed to sell some product for him and had reneged on the deal. He came after her, and that's why she ran. She didn't think I'd be able to protect her."

Duncan slid a notepad and pen at Devin. "Write down the name of this dealer."

She thought maybe Devin would refuse. He didn't. He scribbled down a name and passed it back to Duncan.

Gracelyn's stomach dropped.

Because he'd written *Terry Zimmer.*

"What?" Devin said, obviously noticing her surprise. "You know that guy?"

Now she was the one who hesitated. "How well do you know him?" Gracelyn countered.

"Not well at all, and I want to keep it that way." He leaned back in his chair. "But Zimmer came round a few times before Allie left that first time. I swear, at first I thought the guy was a cop."

"You didn't check out his background or anything?"

Ruston asked. "I mean, since you supposedly have better-than-average computer skills."

Devin's mouth tightened a little. Ruston had obviously managed to get under his skin. A small victory.

"Yeah, I did," Devin admitted. "Former cop turned drug dealer. Talk about a drastic turn in career paths. But other than meeting him a couple of times and checking him on the internet, I don't really know the guy."

"But you saw him with Allie two days ago," Gracelyn reminded him.

"I did, and that's why I wanted to talk to you. I'm worried she's with Zimmer, and if so, God knows what kind of trouble he can get her into."

Gracelyn was worried, too. Especially worried that the trouble involved murder.

"Did you ever hear Allie talk about a man named Marty Bennett?" Gracelyn asked.

"Marty," Devin repeated. "Sure. We both know Marty. Knew," he amended. "I heard he died."

"He was murdered," Ruston provided.

Devin shook his head in an "I'm not surprised" kind of way. "Marty had dealings with a lot of dangerous people."

"So, how did you know him?" Ruston added.

Devin didn't jump to answer this time. "I borrowed money from him twice." He glanced at Gracelyn's raised eyebrow. "I have a trust fund, but sometimes I run short. I paid Marty back every cent, and then some." He paused then. "You think Allie had some kind of run-in with Marty?"

"Did she?" Gracelyn pressed.

"I don't know. Maybe," Devin conceded. Then his eyes widened again. "You don't think she killed him, do you?"

That was the last thing Gracelyn wanted to think. But

she had to consider it. Especially if Allie was truly hooked up with Zimmer.

"Hell," Devin grumbled. "If Allie's gone that far off the rails, I wouldn't let her near the kid. Look, the kid may or may not be mine, but I don't want anything to happen to her, okay?"

"You're not interested in finding out if she actually is your child?" Duncan asked.

Devin shrugged. "If you want me to give you a sample of my DNA, you can check it. I personally don't need the results, but you might want them." He aimed that last part at Gracelyn. "I mean, just in case the kid asks about that sort of thing down the road."

"You don't want to know if she's your daughter?" Gracelyn managed to say, though her throat was very tight now.

"No," Devin insisted. "I'm not exactly the father type. And FYI, I told Allie that when she first suspected she might be pregnant. I told her if she had the kid, it was hers, not mine. I wanted no part of any of that."

Gracelyn hated the way he threw the word *kid* around. Then again, she hated Devin, so it stood to reason she despised anything that came out of his mouth.

"I'll get a DNA test kit," Duncan said, standing.

The surprise flashed through Devin's eyes, but he didn't go back on his offer to give them a sample. Good. This would expedite things. Since Devin had a record, they could go through the database and get his DNA, but this way, his sample could be sent directly to the lab. Then not only could they use the DNA for a paternity test, but they could see if it matched any of the evidence gathered from the multiple crime scenes. It was a long shot, but sometimes long shots paid off.

And that was why she went with another one while Duncan was getting the test.

"Last year your name came up in an investigation that dealt with a black-market baby operation," Gracelyn stated. "You were interviewed because—"

"Because I knew the wrong person," Devin interrupted. He huffed. "Freddy Dundee. I had no idea he was selling babies. And apparently he sold some kids to the so-called baby farm that the cops tried to bust." He stared at her. "You were a cop. Were you involved in the investigation?"

"No," she lied, and she watched his reaction to that. Another of the almost smiles. So, he knew she'd been involved, which meant he likely knew that Ruston had been as well.

"Probably for the best you weren't involved," Devin commented. "I mean, I heard it turned out bad for the cops."

"It turned out bad for the criminals, too," Ruston interjected. "The baby farm was shut down."

"Well, that's good," Devin muttered, and this time there was no reaction at all. Gracelyn wouldn't have wanted to play poker with this guy.

Gracelyn pushed some more. "I'm trying to work out a timeline for Allie and you. When did the two of you become involved?"

"Oh, I've known Allie for years. We met at a party… I'm not sure how long ago. But years, like I said."

"When did you start a romantic relationship with her?" Ruston asked.

Devin shrugged, glanced away. "I'm not sure," he repeated.

"Was it about a year ago?" Ruston pressed. "Longer, shorter?"

Now Devin's eyes hardened. No more poker face. "You're trying to pinpoint if I hooked up with her to get some insider info on the baby-farm investigation. I didn't. And it wasn't a romance. It was sex. Allie tried to make it out to be more than it was." He checked his watch. "Sorry, but I forgot I have another appointment back in San Antonio. Can we wrap this up?"

Gracelyn wanted to continue to push on the baby-farm connection, but Devin seemed right on the edge. She didn't want him walking out, especially before he'd done the DNA test.

"Have you ever had any dealings with Lieutenant Tony Franklin or Detective Charla Burke?" she asked. On the surface, it might seem as if she was changing the subject, but she was just shifting it a little.

Devin repeated the names as if trying to see if they sparked any recognition. He shook his head. "I don't think so, but again, you know I've been arrested." He stopped, smiled. "And I can't recall all the cops involved in every case."

She couldn't tell if he was lying, so she used her phone to pull up photos of both Charla and Tony. And she watched to see if there was any reaction.

Maybe.

There was just a slight tensing of his jaw before he shook his head again. "I don't know them. Why? Are they involved in this mess with Marty?"

Quite possibly. One of them, anyway. But it was equally possible that both Charla and Tony had had nothing to do with the attacks and murders. That could all be on the man sitting directly across from her.

Gracelyn wished there was something they could use to hold Devin while they continued to dig deeper into the investigation. There was his association with Marty. And Allie. But there wasn't any proof that Duncan or SAPD could use for an arrest.

Not yet, anyway.

Duncan came back into the interview room with the test kit, and he handed it to Devin, instructing him on how to use it. Again, Devin hesitated, but he went through with the cheek swab. He handed it back to Duncan and then checked his watch.

"I need to leave for that other appointment," Devin said, standing. "Do any of you have any more questions for me before I go?"

Ruston, Duncan and Gracelyn volleyed glances at each other. It was Duncan who answered. "If we think of anything else, we'll let you know. You'll need to check in with Detective Ryland," he reminded Devin. And he gave Devin the detective's contact information.

"Right. I'll do that." Devin started for the door but then stopped and tipped his head to the test kit Duncan was still holding. "Do me a favor and keep the results of that to yourself," he insisted. "I really don't want to know one way or another if the kid is mine."

He walked out, and for several moments Duncan, Ruston and she sat in silence. No doubt mentally going over everything Devin had just told them. That was what Gracelyn was doing, anyway.

Duncan went to the door and shut it. "You believe him?"

"No," Gracelyn was quick to say. "My gut says he's lying about something. I just don't know what," she admitted.

Duncan made a sound of agreement. "If any part of what he said was true, it doesn't look good for your sister."

"It doesn't," she admitted. "And that's not exactly a surprise. Allie has a history of drug use, and she can be very impulsive. I still don't believe she's a killer, though, and Devin didn't give us any concrete proof that she is."

Duncan tapped the notepad with Zimmer's name on it.

But then he shook his head. "That could be one of Devin's lies. There's no known evidence to indicate Zimmer is a dealer. No known evidence to indicate he's even connected to Allie. I've been digging through Zimmer's background, and nothing about Allie or drugs has come up."

That brought on another round of silence while they obviously thought that through. "So, why would Devin have lied about that?" Gracelyn muttered, and she already had her own theory forming in her head.

"Because Devin might have thought it would make us look at Zimmer and Allie and not him," Ruston threw out. "That way, we might not concentrate on Devin's admission that he knew not only Marty but Zimmer as well."

"And we might not concentrate on the fact that Devin is a known hacker," Duncan spelled out. "A hacker who could have maybe accessed any and all information that was used to murder three people and attack Ruston and you. Added to that, he was interviewed about the baby farm."

All of that was true, but it brought Gracelyn to one very important question. "Why would Devin have killed or hired someone to kill?"

Duncan shrugged. "That's what we need to find out. Maybe this is about money. He worked hard to make it seem as if he wasn't interested in Abigail, but she could be a money source for him. Kidnap her and sell her on the black market. That plan failed, so now he could be in the cover-up mode by implicating Allie." He paused. "But that doesn't explain the two murders of the hacker and retired cop."

Gracelyn could think of an explanation. A bad one. "Devin could be Green Eagle. That would make everything fit."

"Yes," Ruston muttered, and he took out his phone. "I'm calling Noah. I'm hoping he can get Devin in right away and grill him about Marty. And about any possible connection to the baby farm. Noah might be able to get something out of Devin that we missed."

Ruston called Noah, but the detective didn't answer. As Ruston was leaving a voicemail, his phone dinged with an incoming call.

"It's Slater," he relayed.

Every muscle in Gracelyn's body tightened, and she prayed nothing had gone wrong at the ranch.

Ruston quickly finished the voicemail and took the call from his brother on speaker. "Did something happen?" Ruston immediately asked.

"No, everything is secure here," Slater replied just as quickly. "I just got a call, though, from one of the hands. No sign of the sniper, but he found spent shell casings beneath one of those big oak trees near the road. I'll call the CSIs to come out and collect them."

Gracelyn forced herself to unclench some of the tightness in her chest. She knew the exact area of trees that Slater was talking about, and the location probably hadn't been a coincidence. The sniper had likely chosen it so he could make a quick getaway.

"I'll have the CSIs check the ranch trails nearby," Slater went on. "It's possible the gunman parked on one of those and left some tracks."

True, but a former cop like Zimmer would have known that. Then again, Zimmer had left his prints in the truck, so maybe he wasn't careful. There was a third possibility, though, that Zimmer had been set up.

Maybe by Devin.

That could have been why Devin had been so quick to volunteer Zimmer's name to them.

Gracelyn heard a soft sound come from the small bag

she'd brought to the station with her, and it took a couple of seconds for her mind to register what it was.

"It's the alert I set up for messages coming from the private Facebook page," she said, already hurrying to retrieve her phone.

And there it was.

What she'd been waiting for.

It's me, Allie. I don't have the phone you gave me. I must have left it somewhere. Give me your number so I can call you.

Since both Duncan and Ruston had moved closer, she showed them the message, and she fought the urge to fire off a quick response.

"It could be a hoax," she muttered. "Devin or someone else could have gotten access." Still, there was no way she could just ignore this. She typed in her number. And waited.

Gracelyn didn't have to wait long.

Within a couple of seconds, her phone rang, and she saw Unknown Caller on the screen. Holding her breath, she answered it.

"Gracelyn," the caller said, the single word rushing out with a long breath.

"It's Allie," Gracelyn whispered to Duncan and Ruston. The relief came, washing over her. Temporarily, anyway. And then came the worry.

"Allie, where are you?" Gracelyn asked. "Are you all right?"

"No. I'm not all right at all." A hoarse sob tore from her sister's throat. "I'm here in Saddle Ridge, and I have to see you right now."

Gracelyn had so many questions, but she started with an obvious one. "Why are you in Saddle Ridge?"

"I'll tell you when I see you." Allie sobbed again. "When can we meet? I can come to wherever you are."

Gracelyn debated how to respond, and she went with the truth. "I'm at the sheriff's office." She thought that might get Allie to hang up. Or change her mind about meeting with her.

It didn't.

"Okay," Allie finally said. Her voice broke on that single word. "I'll be there in about thirty minutes. I need help, Gracelyn. I need a deal with the cops. I need immunity."

Gracelyn opened her mouth to ask why Allie would need those things, but her sister had already ended the call.

Chapter Nine

Ruston watched Gracelyn pace across the interview room, and he could practically see the nerves coming off her. He was in the same boat, but he was trying to tamp down the worst of his worries.

That this was some kind of ruse for gunmen to try to murder Gracelyn.

Yes, they were in a police station with at least four cops in the building, but if Allie was desperate—and she was a killer—then she might have come here to try to go after her sister.

Ruston had no intention of letting that happen.

Duncan was on the same page with that, because right after Allie had ended her call, he'd gone to his office to let the other deputies know that Allie would be coming in. Or rather she had said she'd be coming in. If she did arrive, she'd be treated like a dangerous suspect and would be thoroughly searched before she got anywhere near Gracelyn.

"Immunity," Gracelyn muttered.

Yeah, Ruston hadn't missed that part. Immunity probably meant Allie had committed a crime and had useful information that she hoped to trade so the cops could catch a bigger fish. But if this was about murder, immunity probably wasn't going to be an option.

And that meant they might have to arrest Allie on the spot.

That thought had no doubt already occurred to Gracelyn, and it had to be contributing to the nerves.

"Has Allie ever been to Saddle Ridge before today?" Ruston asked, hoping the conversation would help settle her before Allie showed up. That thirty-minute arrival was ticking down fast.

"Not that I know of," Gracelyn said, "but I'm sure she heard me mention you were from here."

Yeah, and that meant Allie had made the connection between Gracelyn and him when such a connection shouldn't have been obvious, since before yesterday, they hadn't seen each other in months. But it might have been obvious to Allie if she'd known they had been attacked and had had to flee with Abigail.

One way Allie could have known that was to be directly involved in the attack, but Ruston was hoping that hadn't happened. That instead she'd come by the information from someone else. Like Devin.

"Even though Devin claimed he doesn't know where Allie is," Ruston pointed out, "he could have been lying. He could have been with her when he arranged the meeting and told Allie he was coming here to see us."

Gracelyn nodded, and she seemed to latch on to that. But the hope didn't stay on her face long. Probably because she was well aware of her sister's checkered past. Also, there were those parts about needing immunity and cutting a deal.

There was a knock at the door, and Ruston steeled himself. But it wasn't Allie. It was Woodrow. "There's a cop here to see you. Detective Charla Burke."

Ruston groaned. They didn't need this now. "What does she want?"

"She wouldn't say. Only said it was important."

Ruston connected with Gracelyn's gaze, and even though she didn't look any happier about this intrusion than he was, she nodded. "Let's give her five minutes."

Ruston turned back to Woodrow. "Bring her back here."

That way, Charla wouldn't be in the front of the building when and if Allie came in. After seeing Allie on that surveillance footage, Charla would almost certainly recognize her, and he didn't want the cop trying to question, or intimidate, Gracelyn's sister.

"Duncan probably told you we're expecting another visitor," Ruston commented.

Woodrow nodded. "Allie Wallace. Duncan is keeping an eye out for her."

Good. That was just as they'd planned it since Duncan hadn't wanted Gracelyn in the front of the building either. The windows were bullet resistant, but if the sniper targeted her and used a powerful enough weapon, he might be able to get a shot through. The interview rooms were the only places in the sheriff's office without windows.

"If Allie comes in while Charla is still here, make sure the women's paths don't cross," Ruston spelled out.

"Will do," Woodrow assured him, and he walked away. It didn't take him long to return with Charla.

One look at her face, and Ruston knew she was riled to the bone.

"Make this quick," Ruston immediately told her.

"Quick," Charla snarled like profanity. "Because you're busy trying to ruin Tony's career."

"No." Ruston stretched that out a few syllables. "I'm trying to find out the truth as to why someone has been murdering people. And shooting at Gracelyn, me and you. I know you didn't forget about the sniper."

No way, but it was possible she knew the sniper wasn't an actual threat to her because he was working for her.

"What Internal Affairs is investigating has nothing to do with that," Charla snapped. "It's about some discrepancy in his finances."

"Which could in turn be linked to the attacks and murders," Gracelyn was quick to say. She huffed. "You're a cop, Charla. You know how this works. If there are funds that Tony can't account for, then that opens the door for an investigation into all aspects of his life. Internal Affairs might not find anything."

The anger, and worry, flashed across Charla's face again. "And if they do, it won't have anything to do with murders or attacks."

Yes, but the funds could still be illegal, and that in turn could indeed cost Tony his career.

"I think someone's setting him up," Charla muttered. She fired glances at both Gracelyn and him. "And it sure as hell better not be either of you."

"Or you," Ruston suggested.

Charla practically snapped to attention. "What does that mean?"

Since time was of the essence, Ruston went with a simple response. "Terry Zimmer."

For a couple of seconds, Charla just looked puzzled. Then she put on her cop's face. "What about him?"

"When we showed Tony and you Zimmer's picture, Tony owned up to knowing him," Ruston spelled out. "You didn't."

"Because I—" She stopped, groaned and pinched her eyes together for a second. "I didn't say anything because Zimmer was a confidential informant. And if I'd admitted that, you would have assumed the worst because of the photograph of Zimmer at the baby farm."

"I did assume the worst," Ruston confirmed. "I wouldn't have necessarily done that if you'd been up-front." That was possibly true. Either way, he would have kept Charla on the suspect lists, but she'd made herself look darn guilty by not owning up to knowing Zimmer.

"I swear, I didn't know Zimmer had any connection to the baby farm," Charla insisted.

"But he did," Ruston argued, "and he has a connection to you."

Charla huffed. "You can't possibly believe I was part of that. Why would I? I have no…" She stopped again. "Oh," she muttered. "This is because of my mother."

Bingo.

Charla laughed, but there was no humor in it. "I see. Because my mother sold babies, you believe I continued the family business. I didn't." She paused again. "The only thing I'm guilty of is not admitting I knew Zimmer."

Ruston decided to go out on a limb here. "And protecting Tony. How long have you known about those mystery funds in his accounts?"

Another bingo. Charla certainly didn't jump to deny it, and the look on her face confirmed she had indeed known. "Go ahead, report me to Internal Affairs. Better yet, I'll save you the trouble and do it myself."

Charla stormed out, and Ruston turned to Gracelyn. He didn't get a chance, though, to get her take on everything the woman had just said. That was because his phone dinged with a text.

"It's from Duncan," he said. "Allie just came in, and Duncan has her in his office."

Ruston didn't need to ask for her take on that. She was both relieved and anxious, and she immediately headed out of the interview room. He was right behind her.

When they made it to the front of the building, Charla was thankfully nowhere in sight, which meant she likely hadn't seen Allie. Then again, Ruston might not have seen her either if he hadn't been specifically looking for her. Gracelyn's sister was in the corner of Duncan's office, standing away from the large window, and she was wearing a purple hoodie that covered not only her head but a good portion of her face as well. Her shoulders were hunched, her gaze aimed at the floor.

Duncan was standing by his desk, and the moment Gracelyn and Ruston were inside the office, he shut the door.

"She's been frisked," Duncan told them. "No weapons. And I've already Mirandized her."

If Allie had objected to the frisking and Miranda warning, she didn't voice it. However, when she lifted her head and Ruston got a better look at her face, he could see the agitation in her bloodshot eyes. He searched her face, looking for any resemblance between Gracelyn and her. Or her and the baby. But it just wasn't there.

"Gracelyn," Allie muttered, and the tears came. Probably not her first of the day. "You have to help me."

Gracelyn didn't respond, didn't move. She just stood there for several moments and studied her sister. Then, on a sigh, she went to Allie and hugged her. It didn't last long. Allie ended it and stepped away from her.

"Go ahead," Allie said, defensiveness in her voice now. "Ask me if I've been using. That's what you always do."

"Have you been?" Gracelyn obliged.

"No," Allie snarled. "I'm clean." She paused and groaned. "I haven't used anything today," she amended.

That was possibly true. Possibly. And it drilled home for Ruston that Allie had to be beyond desperate to walk into a sheriff's office and admit that she'd recently used drugs. Something she could be arrested for if they found any illegals in her possession. Then again, she could be arrested for something a whole lot worse.

"You said you wanted immunity," Gracelyn reminded her. "Why? What did you do?"

Allie shook her head and folded her arms over her chest. "First, the immunity, and then I talk."

Gracelyn shook her head. "That's not the way immunity works. You tell us what you know, and then we talk about immunity or a deal."

Allie did more head shaking. "But how do I know you just won't arrest me?" She aimed the question at Duncan.

"You don't, but I could have arrested you the moment you stepped in here, and I didn't," Duncan spelled out. "That's because I want to hear what you have to say. Then I can decide how to help you."

Duncan had clearly sugarcoated that, but Ruston figured if Allie was a victim in all of this, if she had nothing to do with the murders, then Duncan would almost certainly follow through on that "help" if what Allie told them led them to the killer.

"I'll need to record what you say," Duncan added, holding up his phone. "That's for your protection," he said when Allie made a soft gasp. "The district attorney will need to hear your own words before she can work any kind of deal. I can't go to her and just give her a summary."

Not entirely true. Deals happened with summaries. But Duncan wanted anything Allie might say to be on the record. Of course, Allie could lie on the record as well.

"All right," Allie finally said, but she didn't launch into the reason she was here. She sat there until Gracelyn gave her a prompt.

"The San Antonio police have been looking for you," Gracelyn said. She had likely gone with that rather than a direct question to ease Allie into this.

Allie nodded. "I know." She stopped again, and this time she pressed her fingers to her mouth. Both parts of her were trembling, and she looked on the verge of having a full meltdown. "It's because of Marty, isn't it? Because he's dead, and they want to ask me if I killed him. I didn't. I swear, I didn't."

Duncan went to a small fridge behind his desk and brought out a bottle of water for Allie. He also motioned for her to sit in one of the chairs. She drank some water but remained standing.

"You were spotted on a security camera near Marty's around the same time he was killed," Ruston said, figuring it was something Allie might already know.

She did.

"Devin called and told me. He said that's why the cops wanted to talk to me."

Ruston and Gracelyn exchanged glances, and he saw the question in her eyes. Had SAPD released that info about Allie being on the security feed? He shook his head, though that was something that likely would have happened soon if the cops hadn't been able to locate Allie.

So, how had Devin known?

It was something Ruston would have Noah ask Devin if and when the man came back in to be interviewed.

"Why were you at Marty's?" Gracelyn asked her sister.

"Well, it wasn't to kill him," Allie was quick to say. "That'd be like killing the golden goose." She glanced away. "I was going to try to get a loan from Marty. I needed money so I could get back on my feet."

Interesting. "And you knew Marty loaned money because he'd done that for Devin?" Ruston wanted to know.

"Devin," Allie spit out. She said the man's name like profanity. "Yeah, Devin owes Marty lots and lots of money. Some kind of investment deal gone wrong," she added in a mutter.

"Really?" Gracelyn asked. "I was under the impression that Devin had paid off his debts to Marty."

"As if," Allie snarled. "And if Devin told you that, he's lying. Then again, he lies about a lot of stuff." The tears came again, and she sank down into one of the chairs. "He told me he loved me, and then he kicked me out."

Gracelyn sat, too, probably so she'd be eye level with Allie. "Why did he do that?"

Allie stayed quiet for so long that Ruston thought she might just clam up, but she finally answered. "He claimed it was because I used just a little to help take the edge off my nerves. He called me names, said I'd never be anything but a screwup, and he kicked me out. That's why I went to Marty."

Ruston didn't like having to rely on hearsay to try to figure out the big picture here, but it was possible that things had played out that way. If Devin did still owe Marty a lot of money and was trying to resolve that in some way, then he might not have wanted a loose cannon like Allie around.

"Tell me what happened when you went to Marty's," Gracelyn pressed.

Allie drank more water and then took several long breaths. "I saw him twice. First, two days ago, and he was fine then." She had fixed her gaze on her thumbnail now and was scraping away some flakes of bright pink polish. "Then I went back last night to get the money, but Marty was dead when I got there." The water and breaths didn't help. Allie broke into a heavy sob. "He was dead, and there was so much blood. I'd never seen that much blood before."

Ruston got an instant flash of his father's murder. Of the blood. And he relived the shock of seeing that. The crushing pain in his chest that followed. But Ruston shoved that aside. Had to. He had to focus on what Allie was saying to finish creating that mental big picture.

"So, what did you do?" Gracelyn continued.

"I ran, of course," Allie was quick to say. "I got out of there as fast as I could because I thought the killer could still be there. He could have killed me if he thought I was a witness or something."

"He?" Gracelyn questioned. "You thought the killer was a man?"

Allie looked at her and then shook her head. "No. I mean, I didn't know. I just assumed it was a man who'd done something like that. I didn't want to hang around and end up like Marty."

"Or answer questions from the cops who responded to the scene," Duncan commented.

Allie's mouth went into a flat line, but at least she stopped crying. "Or that," she verified, her voice a snap now. "With my record, they would have thought I was responsible, and I'm not."

The cops would have indeed thought that, and Allie would have become their prime suspect with the means and opportunity to have done the kill. But Ruston wasn't sure of her motive.

"Where did you go when you ran from Marty's?" Gracelyn asked.

"To a hotel about six blocks away. I used cash so there wouldn't be a way to trace the room to me."

"Cash?" Gracelyn repeated. "You had cash for a hotel room, but you went to Marty for a loan?"

Allie huffed. "I needed more than what I had on me."

She quickly waved that away as if she didn't want to dwell on that particular subject. "With Marty out of the picture, I decided to try to convince Devin to give me some money. I still had a key to his place, and I slipped in. I wanted to make sure he was in a good mood before I asked him for a loan."

Or she'd slipped in to steal from Devin. But since he didn't want to disrupt the flow of her explanation, Ruston kept that to himself for the moment.

"I heard Devin talking on the phone," Allie went on. "And I heard him say he was coming to Saddle Ridge, and he said all that stuff about me being in trouble." The anger increased with each word. "I knew then he was coming to see you, to whine about me using a little."

"And you followed him?" Gracelyn pressed.

Allie nodded. "I took a taxi, and trust me, that ate up a lot of what little cash I have left, but I didn't want Devin to come here and tell you a bunch of lies about me."

"Why would he do that?" Ruston asked.

"Because he's a selfish SOB, that's why," she was quick to say. "He never once asked about our baby."

Ruston checked the time. Allie had been here for going on ten minutes, and this was the first time she'd brought up Abigail. Added to that, she hadn't mentioned her in the phone call she'd made to Gracelyn.

"So, did Devin tell you lies about me?" Allie asked.

Gracelyn shifted closer to her sister, a signal that she was going to deal with this answer. "He said you were using again and that he kicked you out. He thought you'd hooked up with your former drug dealer."

Allie huffed again. "There was no hooking up. I used, yes, but it was from a small stash I'd left at Devin's last year. I guess he didn't find it, because it was still there."

"Terry Zimmer," Gracelyn threw out there, and she no doubt wanted to groan because she couldn't have missed the flicker of surprise in her sister's eyes.

"I don't know who that is," Allie insisted. It was a lie and not a very good one at that.

"I believe you do," Gracelyn said, somehow managing to keep her voice level. "We've already told you that immunity can't even be considered until you tell us the truth about everything."

"I did tell the truth," Allie howled.

"No, you didn't," Gracelyn argued. "You know Zimmer, and you have to tell me if he's connected to the reason you need immunity."

"I don't know him," Allie practically shouted, springing to her feet. "I don't…" She stopped and locked gazes with Gracelyn, who wasn't pulling a visible punch. She was staring at her sister the way she would a murder suspect.

"The truth," Gracelyn repeated. "That's the only chance you have of me helping you. Lie again, and you'll be arrested."

Allie flung gazes at all three of them, and for a moment, she looked like a trapped animal ready to fight her way out of there. Then a sob tore from her throat, and she sank back into the chair.

"I didn't kill Marty. That's the truth," Allie stated. "And Zimmer isn't my dealer. In fact, I'd never met him until two days ago, when I went to see Marty." She lowered her head, shook it. "You're going to be so upset when you hear this. Really, really upset," she emphasized, "but I swear, at the time I thought it was the only option I had."

Hell. Ruston figured anything that came after this part of the explanation couldn't be good.

"What option?" Gracelyn insisted.

Allie sobbed again, and the tears returned, but thankfully that didn't silence her. "I thought Devin was going to take care of me, but when he didn't, I knew I was going to need some money. A lot of money so I could get away and have a fresh start. I'd heard Marty had connections, so two days ago I went to see him."

Gracelyn pulled in a sharp breath. "Why?" And there was a lot of emotion and strain in that one word.

Allie swallowed hard. "Because I had heard that he sometimes acted as a go-between for people looking to adopt. Good people," she tacked on to that. "I wouldn't want my baby going to just anyone."

Duncan and Ruston both cursed. Hell. She'd planned on selling Abigail.

Gracelyn stayed put in the chair, but her eyes had narrowed. "Say it," she demanded. Not yelling, but there was a dangerous edge to her voice.

"All right." Allie threw an indignant stare right back at her sister. "A couple wanted to adopt the baby, and they were willing to pay my expenses. You know, for carrying her for nine months."

"How much?" Gracelyn asked. That dangerous edge went up a notch.

"Ten thousand," Allie spit out as if she wasn't the least bit ashamed of it. "I knew you wouldn't just hand Abigail over, not without asking me a lot of questions, and I told Marty that. He said there was a way to get her. A fake kidnapping, but it wouldn't actually be a kidnapping because she's my daughter."

Ruston wasn't sure how Gracelyn managed to just sit there and not spew every word of profanity she knew. Maybe because this had shaken her to the core. Allie had been planning on selling that precious baby. And that was just the tip of the iceberg.

Gracelyn held up a hand, maybe to steady herself. Maybe to signal that she wanted to continue the questioning. "How did Marty know where the baby was?"

"I told him. Well, I guessed because I'd seen the file with places where you might be, and I'd taken a picture of it with my phone. You know, just in case I wasn't able to track you down."

So, that was how Marty had gotten the address. Ruston figured Gracelyn was mentally kicking herself for that. All those security precautions down the drain because of Allie.

"You said you saw Zimmer at Marty's," Gracelyn went on a moment later.

"Yes, but not last night, not when I found his body. Zimmer was there on my first visit. I got the impression he worked for Marty. Maybe like an assistant or something."

Ruston was going with the "or something" on this one, and it made him wonder if Zimmer had been around when he'd met with Marty. Maybe. Zimmer certainly hadn't been in the room with them, but it was possible Zimmer had seen him.

"So, how was the fake kidnapping supposed to work?" Duncan asked.

Allie lifted her shoulder. "I'm not sure. Marty said he'd take care of all of that. He just told me to come back when he had the baby and that he'd give me the money. But I didn't want to wait for him to call me. He'd said he'd have the baby last night, so I went to his place to wait."

"Did you know Marty intended for me to be kidnapped as well?" Gracelyn asked.

Allie dismissed that with an eye roll. "That was only so you wouldn't interfere with the men taking the baby. Marty would have let you go."

"Not a chance," Gracelyn muttered. She didn't mutter the rest, though. It came out loud and clear. "You set me up to either die or be sold. You set me up so that I had to fight to save Abigail, Ruston and myself. You did that." She jabbed her index finger at Allie.

Allie huffed once more and got to her feet again. "I did what I had to do to get my daughter. You can't just keep my baby. She's mine, not yours."

Gracelyn stood, too, and, oh, Ruston didn't like that her entire body seemed to make her sister pay. "Yes, biologically you're her mother, and you were planning on selling her. Hear this, Allie—I'll see you locked away for the rest of your miserable life before I let you anywhere near Abigail."

"You can't do that." Allie drew her hand back as if she might slap Gracelyn, but Duncan put a stop to that.

"Sit down and shut up," Duncan ordered Allie.

For a moment, Ruston thought Allie might launch herself at him, but she must have realized that assaulting a cop would only add to the mess she'd gotten herself into.

"I want that deal," Allie snarled. "I want immunity."

"Did you miss that 'shut up' part to my order?" Duncan growled. "Now, sit there and don't say another word until I'm ready for you to talk."

Duncan motioned for them to step out into the bullpen. "You're going to have to turn this over to SAPD, aren't you?" Gracelyn immediately asked him.

"Afraid so." Duncan didn't sound at all pleased about that either. "Every crime she committed, including the most serious ones, are in SAPD's jurisdiction."

Ruston knew that was true, and it was also true that Allie would need to go through this all again with the San Antonio cops. "I'll call Noah," he said. But before he could do that, Woodrow motioned to get his attention.

"You got a call on the station's landline," Woodrow said. "Actually, the caller wants to speak to both Gracelyn and you."

"Who is it?" Ruston asked.

"The guy says he's Terry Zimmer."

Hell. That caused the squad room to go quiet, and there was no need for Ruston to explain to Woodrow who the caller was. Or rather who he was claiming to be. Woodrow and Carmen both knew that was the name of their murder suspect.

"He used your rank, Ruston," Woodrow added. "He knows you're a cop. And he says there are some things you need to know."

Chapter Ten

Zimmer.

Of all the people who she thought might try to contact them, he wasn't one of them. Not unless he wanted to taunt them about the attack. But even if that was Zimmer's intentions, this was a call they had to take.

"Use the landline in the interview room," Duncan offered, glancing back at his office. "And I'll try to have the call traced."

Allie was still in the chair and had moved on to biting her nails instead of just scraping off polish. Just the sight of her made Gracelyn's stomach twist. She would never forgive Allie for trying to sell Abigail. But she'd have to deal with her sister later. For now, she wanted to hear what Zimmer had to say, so Ruston and she headed back to the interview room.

This particular landline had a recording function on it, and Ruston turned that on in the same moment that he answered the call on speaker.

"I'm listening," Ruston said in lieu of a greeting.

"How about Gracelyn?" the man fired back.

Gracelyn didn't think she'd ever heard that voice before. Not a Texas drawl but a quick clip pace that seemed to be void of any accent.

"Gracelyn will especially want to hear what I have to say," the caller insisted.

Ruston motioned for her to stay quiet. And she did. She couldn't think of a good reason to let a murder suspect know her location. It was possible, though, that Woodrow had already done that, but Gracelyn had no intention of confirming it.

"I'll pass along anything you tell me to Gracelyn," Ruston said. "Or you can just turn yourself in, and the three of us can have a face-to-face chat."

Zimmer didn't react to that. "I'm guessing she's there with you," he commented several moments later. "So, I'll just go ahead and direct this to her. And by the way, don't bother with the trace I'm sure you're doing. I'm using a burner."

Gracelyn figured that, but sometimes it was possible to trace the location of a burner. Of course, Zimmer would know that, so he could be either driving around or else planned on leaving the scene as soon as he was done with this call.

"I believe your sister was set up, Gracelyn," Zimmer went on to say. "And, yeah, I know what she tried to do. She wanted to sell her baby. But everything else is a setup."

That could be true. *Could be.* However, the attempt to sell her child and commissioning a double kidnapping wouldn't just end up a slap on the wrist. Allie would be going to jail.

"Did you set Allie up?" Ruston came out and asked.

"No." And there seemed to be genuine frustration in his voice. Zimmer didn't add anything to that, though.

"Then who did?" Ruston demanded.

"I'm not sure. That's the truth," he snapped when Ruston huffed. "At first, I thought it was Marty. I thought maybe he wanted a way out of paying Allie the ten grand he promised her. And maybe it was him and someone then pulled a double cross and put a bullet in his head."

Marty hadn't died from a gunshot to the head but rather to the chest. But Ruston didn't correct Zimmer. It was possible Zimmer already knew that and had doled out some false information so that Ruston and she wouldn't think he was guilty.

Gracelyn didn't buy it, not for a second, and judging from Ruston's expression, neither did he.

"Are you also going to tell me you didn't have any part in trying to kidnap Gracelyn and the baby?" Ruston asked.

Zimmer muttered something she didn't catch. "It's not what you think."

"Then tell me what the hell it was," Ruston snarled.

Gracelyn totally understood the surge of anger in Ruston's voice. The anger raced through her, too, at the thought of how close they had come to dying. And this scumbag was no doubt responsible.

"I've been investigating the baby farm," Zimmer said after a long pause. "Not officially, but I've still got enough cop in me that it doesn't sit well when someone buys and sells babies as if they were merchandise."

"You were working at the baby farm," Ruston pointed out.

"Yeah, so I could dig around and find out who was responsible. I wanted to bring him or her down. I wanted to put an end to it."

Ruston didn't appear ready to tamp down his anger or the sarcasm that went along with it. "You seem awfully dedicated to justice, considering you're a disgraced former cop. Or do you have an excuse for that, too? Maybe someone set you up?"

"No. I used excessive force, and I resigned." There was some anger in his tone now, too. "And I'm dedicated to justice in this particular matter because when I was a baby, I was sold to a couple in a private adoption. A couple who shouldn't have been given a pet rock, much less a kid."

Ruston used his cell to open the site where records of former police officers could be accessed. He used his password to access it and then handed Gracelyn his phone so she could check and see if there was anything in Zimmer's background to indicate there was a shred of truth in what he was saying.

"Because I wanted to find the person running the baby farm, I managed to get hired as a security guard," Zimmer went on. "Just like Gracelyn and you did."

Oh, that reminder didn't help ease any of Ruston's anger. Nor hers. "Were you the one who tried to kill Gracelyn and me that night, just like you did when you attempted to kidnap the baby and her?"

"No." Zimmer paused and repeated that through what sounded to be clenched teeth. "I don't know who shot at you at the baby farm. And I didn't shoot at you during the kidnapping attempt either. Yes, I fired shots, but I purposely aimed away from you. That was to convince the thug who was with me that he and I were on the same side. If he'd thought I had my own reasons for being there, he would have killed me."

Ruston paused a moment, probably to try to wrap his mind around all of that and figure out if it was true. While he did that, Gracelyn showed him what she'd accessed on Zimmer. There were no accounts of any childhood abuse. No reported accounts, anyway, but Zimmer was a former elementary school counselor, and when he'd been on the force, he'd routinely volunteered to work with troubled kids who'd ended up in juvie.

Another thing stood out, though.

The excessive-force charge had involved a couple who had gotten off child-abuse charges because of a botched investigation. Zimmer had been the investigator.

All of that presented a package of a man who seemed to want to help kids and get them away from scumbag parents. But that didn't mean Zimmer hadn't crossed some very big lines and turned criminal.

"Give me the name of the thug who was with you when you attacked Gracelyn and me," Ruston ordered.

"He used the name Buddy Bradley," Zimmer answered without hesitation. "Marty said Buddy had worked for him for years. I'm guessing the CSIs found his blood in the truck and sent it to the lab. If you don't have confirmation already, you'll soon get it and learn his real name was Robert Radley and that he had a record a mile long."

"Was? Had?" Ruston questioned as Gracelyn started looking for any info on him.

"He's dead. And, no, I didn't kill him," Zimmer insisted. "You did. Or maybe it was Gracelyn. Whoever fired that shot at him through the door. The bullet must have nicked an artery or something, because by the time I got him in the backup vehicle we'd left on one of those ranch trails, he'd bled out."

Gracelyn held up his phone so he could see the quick run she'd just done on Robert Radley. The man was forty-two and did indeed have a long criminal history that included B and E, assault and drug charges. He'd been in and out of jail since he was sixteen.

"I'd never met Buddy before Marty paired us up to do

the kidnapping," Zimmer went on. "But it took me about a half of a second to realize he was a dangerous hothead."

"And yet you went through with the job," Ruston reminded him.

Zimmer was quick to answer that, too. "If I hadn't, Marty would have just hired someone else. I figured if I was there, I could keep Buddy in check. Obviously, I failed at that."

"Yeah, you did," Ruston agreed. "Now, tell me why the hell Marty hired you and the hothead when he had already arranged for someone else to kidnap Gracelyn and the baby."

That was the big question, and Gracelyn automatically moved closer to the landline because she didn't want to miss a word of this.

"You," Zimmer said. "Marty hired you to do the kidnapping." He groaned. "I was at Marty's when he called you over. Marty asked that I stay out of sight in a little room he has off his office. He wanted me to listen to the conversation and make sure there were no red flags in anything you were saying. He wasn't sure he could trust you."

The muscles in Ruston's jaw turned to iron. "Did you recognize me?"

"I did," Zimmer admitted. "I'd gotten copies of the reports on the baby-farm attack, and I knew you were there. Gracelyn, too."

"Did your friend Charla get you those copies?" Ruston asked.

"No. I, uh, hired someone for that." Zimmer's voice lowered to a murmur. "A hacker. Simon Milbrath, and yeah, I know it looks bad that he was murdered, but I didn't kill him."

Gracelyn saw the mountain of skepticism in Ruston's expression. She was right there with him. So far, Zimmer had what was called the *categorical trinity*. Means, motive and opportunity. Zimmer could have killed both Marty and Simon to eliminate anyone who could have ratted him out. And since Zimmer had already admitted to hiring a hacker, that same hacker could have been keeping tabs on anything connected to the baby-farm investigation. The call Archie made to Tony might have fallen into that category.

"You told Marty I was a cop," Ruston said.

"I told him I thought you were an informant for the cops," Zimmer corrected as if that were a good thing. "And I did that, hoping that Marty would pull you off the assignment."

"Why? Because you knew I'd kill you for coming after Gracelyn and the baby?" Ruston's voice was pure ice now.

"No. I did it because I could tell Marty was suspicious of you. Why else have me listen in on the conversation? Marty didn't fully trust you, and I figured it was safer for you to be pulled off the job rather than risk Marty having you killed."

"That's generous of you," Ruston countered. "And why was Marty suspicious of me? Because of something you told him?"

"I think Allie must have said something about you, like maybe you could have helped Gracelyn go into hiding. If Allie had mentioned you, Marty would have looked you up. Hell, Marty had hackers on his payroll, and he could have discovered you were a cop and set you up to die. Marty didn't come out and say that to me, but Buddy was awfully fast on the trigger."

Ruston and she locked gazes, no doubt so he could see what her take was on this. Gracelyn had to shake her head. Like Allie, Zimmer wasn't innocent. He was a criminal, but maybe he hadn't gone to her place with the intention of killing anyone.

"Did Marty break into my apartment?" Ruston asked Zimmer.

"I'm not sure. When I showed up to do the job, Buddy had your wallet, and he said Marty had told him to leave it at Gracelyn's."

"And my badge?" Ruston added.

"I don't know about that," Zimmer answered. "If Marty or Buddy had it, they didn't share that info with me."

Again, Gracelyn had no idea if that was the truth. She was betting Ruston didn't either.

"Someone fired shots at an SAPD cruiser," Ruston said. "Was that you?"

Zimmer muttered some profanity. "It was," he verified and then paused. "After Marty was murdered, I got a call from a guy who said he was Marty's partner and that he had one last job for me. No, I don't have a name. He wouldn't say, but he told me he had photos and recordings of me with Marty from when I agreed to kidnap Gracelyn and the baby. He said he'd turn that over to the cops if I didn't do one last job."

"The job of trying to shoot the two police officers in that cruiser," Ruston snapped.

"No, the job of firing shots at the cruiser. The man told me to miss. I wouldn't have done it otherwise."

Ruston's gaze met hers. "Was Marty's partner your old friend Tony?" he asked Zimmer.

"No," the man repeated. "That wasn't him on the phone. I think I would have recognized his voice."

"Think?" Ruston challenged.

Zimmer stayed quiet for a while. "I don't believe it was him." Then he stopped and cursed. "Maybe it was. Anyway, I agreed to go through with it with one stipulation. That the so-called partner meet me in person afterward and hand over those photos and recordings. I had to figure the guy would keep copies and would continue trying to use them as leverage for future jobs, but I wanted that meeting to know who I was dealing with."

"And?" Ruston prompted when Zimmer fell silent.

"He didn't show for the meeting. And he hasn't contacted me since."

The partner could be Tony. Or Charla, for that matter, if she'd gotten a man to make that call for her. Devin could have done it as well.

"What is it you want me to do with what you've just told me?" Ruston continued a moment later.

"I want you to find out who killed Marty, Simon and the retired cop," Zimmer was quick to say. "And it wasn't Allie. Find out who it was, and I'll turn myself in. If I do that now, I'll end up dead. Find the killer," he insisted a split second before he ended the call.

Ruston ended the recording, and he immediately called Duncan. "Were you able to get a trace?" he asked.

"No," Gracelyn heard Duncan say.

And then she heard something else. Something that sent her stomach to her knees.

A woman screamed.

"Allie," Gracelyn said, her sister's name rushing out with her breath.

Ruston threw open the interview room door. In the same motion, he put away his phone and started running toward Duncan's office. Gracelyn was right behind him. They raced into the squad room.

And into chaos.

Allie was still in Duncan's office. Still screaming. Gracelyn soon saw why. There were two uniformed officers, and both had their weapons drawn. One of them, a beefy black-haired man, had Deputy Carmen Gonzales in a choke hold, and his Glock was pointed at her head. The other man, a lanky blond guy, was aiming at Allie.

He fired.

Just as Duncan tackled Allie and knocked her to the ground. The shot crashed through the office window, causing the glass to explode, but Gracelyn couldn't tell if the bullet had hit her sister. Or Duncan.

Ruston drew his gun. So did Gracelyn. Just as the lanky blond man turned his weapon toward them. Ruston dragged her to the floor as he fired.

There was the howl of some kind of alarm, loud and blaring, and Gracelyn saw Woodrow beneath his desk, where he'd taken cover. Either Duncan or he must have activated a security alert, and she hoped that brought officers responding to the scene. They might not get there in time.

Another shot came their way, blasting into the wall mere inches above their heads.

Mercy, what was happening? Gracelyn didn't have a full answer to that, but one thing was for certain. These weren't good cops. They might not even be cops at all, and they had probably used their uniforms and badges to gain access to the building.

And Allie, Ruston and she were their targets.

She cursed the call that'd just come from Zimmer. He'd phoned the landline, maybe to make sure they were there so he could send in these goons. If so, it'd been beyond gutsy to have hired guns come into a police station.

Gutsy and maybe extremely effective.

Ruston and she had a small amount of cover since there was a desk in front of them, but if the blond shooter came closer, he'd basically have them pinned down. That was probably why Ruston maneuvered himself in front of her. Shielding her. And in doing so, he was putting himself in the direct line of fire.

Gracelyn didn't want Ruston sacrificing himself for her, but this wasn't the time for her to question what he was doing. And what he was doing was getting himself into a better position to fire if he got a clean shot. At the moment, he didn't have one since both gunmen were using Carmen as their shield.

"Stop them," Allie yelled. "They're going to kill all of us."

Her sister might be right. If these fake cops had come here to eliminate Ruston, Allie and her, then they weren't likely to leave Duncan, Carmen or Woodrow alive either.

"They've locked the front door," Ruston whispered to her.

That didn't help her tamp down the wild surge of adrenaline. It meant no responders would be coming in that way. But there were other doors to the sheriff's office, and she doubted they'd managed to lock them all.

Around the squad room, phones began to ring, the sounds blending with the loud, pulsing alarm. Responders were probably trying to find out what was going on, but no one answered any of the phones. Well, maybe Duncan did. Gracelyn couldn't see Allie or him.

"If you want to save some lives, step out and let's finish this," the bulky gunman growled.

Gracelyn didn't have any doubts about what he meant. He wanted Ruston, Allie and her to sacrifice themselves. And she might have considered it. Might. But she went back to her original idea. These gunmen had no intentions of letting any of them live.

"Keep watch behind us," Ruston muttered.

That slammed her with more adrenaline, but she turned so she was essentially back-to-back with him. And got the mother lode of flashbacks. To survive the attack at the baby farm, they'd had to do this. They'd had to sit there with the threat of being gunned down and dying.

Gracelyn shook her head, forcing back those images. Forcing back the gut-wrenching emotions that went along with them. She couldn't let those flashbacks play into what was happening now. She just couldn't. Because it could get a whole lot of people killed.

"Five seconds," the gunman warned them. "That's how long you've got before we start shooting the hell out of this place. We won't kill Deputy Gonzales right off, but we'll make her wish she was dead."

Gracelyn couldn't see Carmen's face, but she knew the woman had to be terrified as the gunman started the countdown.

"Five…"

Ruston inched closer to the side of the desk. From Duncan's office, Allie quit screaming, making Gracelyn wonder if she had been hit after all. Or maybe Duncan had just figured out a way to silence her.

"Four…"

Gracelyn kept watch of the hall and the sides of the room, and from the corner of her eye, she saw Woodrow move as well. Like Ruston, he was adjusting his position, preparing for an attack.

"Three… Time's running out," the gunman added as a threat.

Woodrow looked in their direction, and even though Gracelyn couldn't see Ruston's face, he nodded. Woodrow and he had made some kind of silent pact. Maybe to leave cover and try to get that clean shot.

Gracelyn decided to help with that.

"Two," the gunman barked out.

She took off one of her shoes, holding it for a split second in Ruston's line of sight so he'd know what she was doing. Then she hurled it over the desk and in the direction of Carmen and the gunmen.

All hell broke loose.

There were scuffling sounds, and shots rang out. So many shots. With the alarms and the blasts, she couldn't tell what direction the gunfire was coming from, but it seemed to be coming from everywhere at once.

And maybe it was.

She caught a glimpse of Duncan crouched down in the doorway. Ruston and Woodrow had left cover and were both firing. Gracelyn continued to keep watch behind them, but she scrambled around to the side of the desk and saw Carmen on the floor. The deputy didn't appear to have been shot, but she was crawling toward Gracelyn.

The blond gunman pivoted to shoot Carmen, but he didn't get the chance. Gracelyn fired, but she was pretty sure that Woodrow and Ruston did as well. Maybe even Duncan. Multiple shots hit the gunman in the chest, and he dropped like a stone, his weapon clattering to the floor.

The beefy gunman dropped, too, but he wasn't shot. He was coming after Carmen, no doubt to get back his human shield.

He failed.

There was another round of gunfire. Gracelyn couldn't get in on this one because Carmen was in front of her, but her shot wasn't necessary. Bullets slammed into the gunman, and he used his last breath to snarl out some profanity. Gracelyn figured he was dead before he even hit the floor.

Gracelyn continued to hold her breath. Continued to

watch for another attacker. Someone, maybe Woodrow, shut off the alarm, but around the office, the phones continued to ring.

"Is anyone hurt?" Duncan called out.

"I'm okay," Carmen answered.

Gracelyn didn't answer. Couldn't. Because she couldn't unclamp her throat enough to speak. She just wanted to hear Ruston's voice. She needed to know he was okay.

"I'm fine." That came from Woodrow. "Are you hurt?"

"No," Duncan confirmed.

"I'm okay," Ruston finally said. "Gracelyn?"

"Okay," she finally managed. The relief came. Well, relief about Ruston and the others, anyway.

"Allie, were you hit?" Gracelyn called out.

Nothing.

No response.

Not for a couple of seconds, anyway, and then she heard Duncan curse. "Allie's not here."

Alarmed, Gracelyn stood, her gaze zooming to Duncan's office. Since the glass was now gone, she had no trouble seeing directly inside. And what she saw was the open side door that her sister had almost certainly used to escape.

Chapter Eleven

Ruston seriously doubted Gracelyn was actually sleeping, but since she wasn't saying anything, he stayed quiet as well.

And replayed every second of the nightmare that'd happened at the sheriff's office.

That'd been over twelve hours ago, and after the shots had ended, both Gracelyn and he had gotten caught up in the investigative whirlwind of trying to piece everything together. That had been both an exhausting and frustrating process that was merely on pause so everyone could get some rest.

In Gracelyn's and his case, they'd chosen for that "rest" to happen at the ranch so she could be with Abigail. Ruston had even managed to get Gracelyn to eat something before they'd gone to bed. Well, she had gone to bed, and he'd taken the chair again. She had offered to share the queen-size bed with him, and that'd been a damn tempting offer, but he didn't have a lot of willpower right now when it came to Gracelyn. What could start as a hug of comfort could turn into a whole lot more, and Gracelyn didn't need that right now.

Like him, she needed some rest so she could approach the investigation with a clear head.

Clearly, Duncan wasn't in the rest mode, because even though it was well past midnight, Ruston's phone lit up with a text from him. Ruston had put his cell on silent, even shutting off the vibration so that it wouldn't wake Gracelyn if she did indeed manage to fall asleep. But she must have seen the flash of light, because she sat up, her gaze racing across the room to him.

"Did they find Allie?" she whispered.

The only light was coming from the ajar bathroom door, but Ruston had no trouble seeing that she was not only wide-awake but that she was just as on edge as he was.

He shook his head. "Duncan got IDs on the two dead fake cops, though. And they were fake," he emphasized, trying to keep his voice as low as possible. Abigail was only an hour into what should be a three- or four-hour stretch of sleep for her, and he didn't want to disturb her.

Apparently, Gracelyn was concerned about disturbing Abigail, too, because she moved as if to get out of bed to come to him. Ruston fixed that by going to her. He sat on the edge of the bed so they could talk, but he hoped this would be a short conversation. He was still hanging on to the hope that Gracelyn might actually get some rest tonight.

She wasn't wearing the pajamas that Joelle had brought in for her but had opted for a loose pair of loaner jogging pants and a T-shirt. Her shoes were right next to the bed beside her freshly restocked go bag. All indications she was ready to get Abigail out of there if necessary.

Ruston was hoping like the devil it wouldn't be necessary.

"The dead men are Eddie Baker and Andre Culpepper," Ruston told her. "Both have criminal records. According to Carmen, when they showed up to escort a prisoner to Austin, she thought there was something suspicious about the paperwork they had. She was about to call Austin PD when one of them grabbed her."

That was a nutshell account of what'd happened. Of course, the emotional couldn't be put in a nutshell. There'd been an attack at the sheriff's office, and now two men were dead. No wonder Duncan was still at work.

"What about the prisoner they were supposed to transport?" Gracelyn asked. "Was he in on it?"

"Duncan doesn't think so. Austin PD was actually sending down two officers to collect him, but they weren't coming for another two hours."

She stayed quiet for several seconds. "So, these two fake cops would have had access to Austin PD info," she concluded.

"Looks that way," he agreed.

"Zimmer," she muttered. "He could have set all of this up."

She'd get no argument from him about that. In fact, it was possible Zimmer had orchestrated this and everything else that'd happened. The man had sounded somewhat sincere when he'd told them about his quest to catch those involved in the baby farm, but that could have been all smoke. A ruse to confirm Gracelyn and he were at the sheriff's office so he could send in the thugs to attack.

"We were the targets," she said. "Me, you and Allie. They came there to kill us." Her voice broke and she squeezed her eyes shut as if trying to hold back tears.

Cursing and breaking his promise to himself that he wouldn't try to soothe her, Ruston pulled her into his arms. A hug probably wasn't going to do much, but it was all he had. There was no good news to give her. Heck, he couldn't even dispute that part about them being targets. In fact, it all made sense if Zimmer was trying to tie up some loose ends.

"I'm not going to let Allie or Zimmer get to Abigail," she whispered, her words brushing against his neck.

Ruston rethought that notion about a hug not doing much good because Gracelyn sounded stronger than she had just seconds earlier. Of course, the baby could do that. Ruston would protect the little girl with his own life, and that included not letting Allie or Zimmer get anywhere near her.

"Allie doesn't even love her," Gracelyn went on. "She was going to sell her."

"I know," Ruston murmured. And he knew something else.

That Gracelyn did love the baby.

Heck, so did he. That added even more urgency to the need to keep Gracelyn and her safe.

"Has there been any sign of Allie?" she asked.

"No." And that had given him plenty to think about.

If Allie had told the truth about not having much money, she couldn't have gotten far. Not on her own, anyway. But it was possible Zimmer or another thug was waiting near the sheriff's office and scooped her up after she ran outside. If that hadn't happened, then whoever had hired those two fake cops would no doubt be looking for her.

If they found her, they'd kill her.

Ruston knew Gracelyn was well aware of that. Allie probably was, too, but so far, that hadn't caused Allie to seek out police protection, something she could get with one phone call to either Gracelyn, Duncan or him.

Gracelyn had left a message for Allie encouraging her to do just that. To accept that protection. But so far, there'd been no response from her sister.

She eased back from him, just far enough for her to make eye contact. "You moved in front of me," she said, and he must have looked confused, because she added, "During the shooting."

Oh, that. "Yeah," he admitted. "It has nothing to do with you being a woman. It was just instinct."

Since she wasn't exactly doling out any thanks, he geared up to add an apology to that. And let her know that his instincts would be the same if it happened again.

"You did that at the baby farm, too," she muttered.

Ruston couldn't recall that for certain. Those moments they'd been pinned down by gunfire were a blur. Then again, he'd worked hard to make sure they were. He didn't need images like that in his head.

She sighed. "What's going on here?" Gracelyn asked.

And he didn't think they were talking about gunfire any longer. Nope. There was just enough light for him to see the change in her eyes. Her breath hitched a little. He felt her muscles tense beneath his hands. A reminder that he was still holding her in his arms.

"I think what's going on is a complication," he admitted. "Something we'd like to postpone. But it doesn't seem to want to go away."

"No," she quietly agreed.

They sat there, face-to-face, body-to-body, and it seemed as if everything stopped. Only for a second or two. But in that brief span of time, Ruston managed to have an argument with himself as to why he should move away from her.

An argument he lost.

Gracelyn lost it, too, because she was the one who leaned in and pressed her mouth to his. And just that, just that brief touch of her lips, sent the heat soaring.

He tried to rein in that heat. That need. But it was a lost cause and not one he wanted to win. He wanted to kiss Gracelyn, so that was exactly what he did.

She moaned, the silky sound one of pleasure, and immediately notched up the intensity by deepening the kiss.

The taste of her hit him hard again, spearing right through him and instantly making him want more.

He took more.

Ruston tightened his grip on her and brought her closer to him. Until her breasts were against his chest. Until there was no space or distance between them. And even that didn't seem close enough.

Of course, his body was insisting on getting closer to her. His body was urging him on and on. And Gracelyn certainly wasn't putting on the brakes either. So, maybe she was using this to shut out the nightmarish thoughts if even for a minute. Maybe this was a kind of comfort after all.

That notion stayed with him until she skimmed her hand down his back and then snuggled even closer to him, adjusting her position until she was in his lap. The kiss didn't stop. It continued to rage on. So did the touching, and Ruston got in on that. He slid his fingers over her breasts. And enjoyed the hell out of that little hitch that came from her throat.

This was how things had started the night after the baby-farm attack. The hug that had led to a kiss. The kiss that had led to, well, a hot and heavy make-out session that had landed them in bed. Since they were already in bed, they wouldn't have far to go.

But was Gracelyn ready for this?

Physically, yeah, she was. He could feel the unspoken invitation she was offering him. However, going just the physical route here could cause her to have lots of regrets. That was what had happened last time, and it had sent her running. Ruston didn't want that again.

And that was why he pulled back from her.

Not easily. It took every bit of willpower he could muster, and even then, he wasn't sure it was a battle he was going to win with himself. If she'd kissed him again, that would snap the leash on the heat, and they would just have to deal with things like regret later.

But she didn't kiss him.

She didn't move off his lap either, and he was well aware that the center of her body was pressing against his erection.

Gracelyn stared at him. "I want you to know that after the shooting at the baby farm, I didn't leave because of you. I left because of me, because I couldn't stay and deal with what was going on in my head."

"I understand," he assured her. And he did. "There were times after my father was killed when I considered leaving for a while, too."

"But you stayed because of your siblings," she finished for him.

He nodded. Joelle and Bree had taken the murder so hard. Heck, they all had, but they had found strength with each other. Gracelyn hadn't had that with Allie.

"Once this is over and the killer is caught, we should go on a date," she said.

Ruston laughed and then immediately cut off the sound when Abigail squirmed a little. He waited until he was sure she was back asleep before he responded.

"I'd like to go on a date with you," he told her and brushed his mouth over hers again. Not a hungry kiss exactly, but then again, with Gracelyn, hunger was always right beneath the surface.

She snapped it straight to the surface when she leaned in and kissed him again. The real deal kiss.

Nothing held back.

And considering they were both already hot and primed, Ruston knew exactly where this was going.

GRACELYN FIGURED THIS was a huge mistake, but she simply didn't care. She wanted Ruston. Needed him. And she didn't have the willpower to fight off that need any longer. She just sank into the kiss and let Ruston and his incredible mouth perform some magic.

The magic happened, all right.

She felt the heat race through her, and Gracelyn just let it carry her away. It had been like this on that other night Ruston and she had been together. That one, too, had been fueled with spent adrenaline and need. So much need. And once again, Ruston managed to notch up the heat.

They were already face-to-face, body-to-body, center-to-center, and that made it easier for him to lower his mouth to her neck and light some fires there. He touched, too. Mercy, did he touch. There was an urgency, and a gentleness, in the way he slid his hand down her back.

Gracelyn nearly got lost in the fiery haze, nearly let Ruston carry her away. But she wanted to give as good as she was getting. She wanted to do her own tasting and touching, so she unhooked his shoulder holster, setting the weapon aside on the nightstand, and then rid him of his shirt.

And her version of touching and tasting began.

She lowered her head, kissed his chest, and she felt his muscles stir beneath her mouth. Gracelyn used her tongue. Heard the rumble of pleasure that came deep from within his throat. She kept kissing while she slid her hand to his stomach.

More muscles stirred. He made that sound again. And she just kept pushing, firing up the heat. Until Ruston could seemingly take no more. He pulled off her top and turned the tables on her by touching her breasts. It was an amazing sensation that became so much more when he rid her of her bra.

The urgency escalated. Of course it did. This level of heat couldn't last, and it demanded to be sated now. That was the word pounding through her head—*now*—when she reached for the zipper of his jeans. He stopped her, and Gracelyn muttered some profanity when he moved her off his lap and stood.

For a few horrible moments she thought he was stopping, but Ruston pulled off his boots before he fished through the pocket of his jeans and came out with his wallet. Then a condom.

Gracelyn wanted to curse some more because the heat and need had nearly made her forget the whole safe-sex thing. Thankfully, Ruston hadn't. Also, thankfully, he was prepared.

And naked.

That happened when he shucked off his jeans and boxers. A fully clothed Ruston could fire her up, but a naked one stole her breath. The man was drop-dead hot, and he was hers.

Well, hers for this moment, anyway.

And this moment was enough. Gracelyn wouldn't allow herself to think beyond it. She didn't want to deal with anything but this urgency that was building, building, building in every inch of her.

Ruston moved back toward the bed, anchoring his knee on the edge of the mattress while he leaned in and pulled off her sweatpants. And panties. He didn't lower on top of her, though. But he kissed her. A long, slow slide of his mouth that started at her neck and went lower. To her breasts.

Then lower. To her stomach.

Then lower still. And that was a kiss that had Gracelyn jolting. That had her nearly flying right over the edge of a climax. While she was certain that would be amazing, she didn't want to finish things like this.

She levered herself up, not easily, and took hold of Ruston to pull him down on top of her. She wanted his body on hers. And that was what she got. She wanted him to be as mindless and ready as she was, and she got that, too, when she wrapped her hand around his erection.

Judging from the profanity he grumbled, that was the best kind of torture for him, and it caused him to hurry to get the condom on.

They were face-to-face again when he pushed inside her. Face-to-face when the thrusts turned from gentle and testing to deep and demanding. Face-to-face when those thrusts made it impossible for her to hang on any longer.

Gracelyn let him finish her. She let Ruston take her to the only place she wanted to go.

With the climax rippling through her, they were face-to-face when she kissed him and took Ruston right along with her.

Chapter Twelve

Ruston lay next to Gracelyn while she slept. And she was indeed sleeping. He could tell from the now gentle, even rhythm of her breathing. Nothing like the urgent pace that'd happened when they were having sex. Then again, there were many things that took on that level of heat and need.

There weren't many things that could make him forget that a killer was after them. Temporarily forget, anyway. Now that the fire had been cooled for the moment, he remembered.

And he worried.

How the hell was he going to keep Abigail and Gracelyn safe?

For the moment they didn't have anyone trying to gun them down, but Ruston also knew they couldn't stay holed up like this. It was like being undercover. With a baby, no less. That had to stop.

But how?

He didn't even know who was trying to kill them, much less how to draw the person out in a way that didn't involve putting Gracelyn or Abigail in even more danger than they already were.

There was one bright thing in all of this. Gracelyn and he were fully on the same side now. They were together, and while he wasn't going to try to figure out what that meant for the future, Ruston knew they'd be working together to protect Abigail.

"I can practically hear you thinking," Gracelyn muttered.

Ruston silently cursed when he looked down and saw she was now wide-awake. He silently cursed again at the heat that instantly notched up inside him just by looking at her.

"I was hoping you'd get more than an hour's sleep," he said, and because he couldn't stop himself, he kissed her.

Gracelyn kissed him right back and made that amazing sound of pleasure that took the hunger up even more. And while his body was all for revving up, it wasn't a good idea.

"I don't have a second condom," he told her.

She winced a little, then smiled. A wistful kind of smile that had an edge to it. The kind of edgy vibe that lovers threw off when the heat was strong and wouldn't just go away.

Using a single finger, she slid a strand of hair off his forehead. That shouldn't have felt like foreplay. It did. Then again, at the moment her breathing felt like foreplay, too.

He kissed her, way too long, way too deep. Enough to fire them both up. He would have taken that heat to the center of her body for some very pleasurable kisses. But a flash of light stopped him.

It hadn't come from the window, so it wasn't headlights. It took him a second to realize it was the phone. It was on the floor mixed with their discarded clothes. And it grabbed his attention, all right. It grabbed Gracelyn's, too, because she tensed, clearly bracing for the worst.

He scrambled off the bed, located the phone and saw the name on the screen. "It's a text from Luca," he relayed to her.

Apparently, Luca wasn't getting any sleep tonight either.

Ruston read the message and quickly told her so she could release the breath she was holding.

"The search team found the dead man, Buddy, who Zimmer told us about," Ruston explained. "The body was just off one of the ranch trails. The medical examiner will get the body and give us a cause of death, but Luca says it appears the guy did bleed out. So, Zimmer hadn't lied about that."

But Ruston immediately rethought that.

"Zimmer could have been the one to kill him," Ruston amended. "I could have shot Buddy when he was at the front door of your house, but Zimmer could have finished him off. Zimmer might not have wanted to leave behind a loose end, especially one who's a hothead."

Obviously, that hadn't occurred to Gracelyn yet, but it would have soon enough. Zimmer could have told them only the details that would paint him in the best light possible. The bottom line, though, was Zimmer could be a cold-blooded killer.

"Duncan will look for any connection between Zimmer and the dead fake cops," Ruston assured her. Since it didn't feel right to be discussing this while he was naked, he began to dress. "But my guess is if there is one, it won't be obvious. Whoever set this up had to know it was risky."

She made a sound of agreement and must have felt the same way he did, because she got up and started dressing as well. "And yet he went through with the plan anyway." Gracelyn sighed. "That tells me the attacks aren't going to stop." She pulled on her top, and when she'd gotten her head through the neck opening, she looked him straight in the eyes. "You and I are the ultimate loose ends because the killer has to know we won't stop until he's caught."

Ruston couldn't argue with any of that, but he had a bad

feeling about where Gracelyn was going with this. Still, he sat there and heard her out.

"Before today, I thought Abigail was the target," she continued. She pulled on her panties and then the jogging pants. "But I think they wanted her only because they could sell her. They didn't come after her here at the ranch. Thank God," she added in a mutter. "They came after us instead. So, we're their priority."

Again, he couldn't argue. In fact, he could take this line of thought one step further. "You're thinking Abigail would be safer away from us."

She nodded, but he saw the dread that was causing. For all intents and purposes, Gracelyn had become Abigail's mother, and it would crush her to have to leave the baby. Still, it would crush her even more if Abigail was hurt because some thugs were coming after Ruston and her.

But there was even more to this.

More that had Ruston muttering some profanity.

"You're thinking of making ourselves bait," he spelled out. He cursed while he finished putting on his clothes and his shoulder holster.

"Bait with a plan," she said, and she continued talking despite his groan. "We could leave Abigail here with lots of protection. Lots," she emphasized. "I mean security that's so tight, there's no way anyone can get to her. Then you and I could draw out the killer. Because as you know, we'll never be safe until the killer is caught."

He did know that. But there was a part of this plan he didn't like, and that was a huge understatement.

"You could have that same airtight security," Ruston insisted. "You could be here with Abigail, and I could become the bait."

She stared at him and took hold of his shoulders. "They

want both of us, Ruston. If I'm here, they could come here. Or they just wait until something draws me out. I can't stay holed up in here forever, and they know that."

Ruston wanted to argue with her. Mercy, he did. Because he wanted to keep Gracelyn safe. He didn't want her anywhere near the line of fire again.

"We've done undercover together before," she added a moment later, "and this would be very similar."

"Yeah, and the last time we were undercover together, we nearly died," he reminded her.

"Because someone betrayed us or made us as cops. Maybe Zimmer. Maybe Charla or Tony. Heck, maybe it was Devin, since he seems to be connected to everything that's happening. But for this, we make the plan. This time, only people we trust will know what's going on."

That would be a given, but he still wasn't on board. "So, what? We set up somewhere and lure the killer to us? Because he won't be alone. And, heck, might not come at all. He could send more hired thugs like he did at the sheriff's office."

"He might be running out of hired thugs," she muttered. "But if he's not, then the plan should include capturing at least one of them and getting him to talk."

Ruston huffed because there were so many things that could go wrong with this plan, and Gracelyn no doubt saw the skepticism that was still all over his face.

"Let's map it out like an op," she went on. "Then we can identify any weak spots and fix them. Only then do we go in. Only then do we put this into motion."

"And what if the op is mapped out, and there are weak spots we can't eliminate?" he asked.

"Then we come up with another plan, one where we can make it as safe as possible."

Which wouldn't be very safe if they were literally putting themselves out there as bait. Unfortunately, he thought the bait would work. The killer seemed desperate to eliminate them. Still...

His phone lit up again, and this time, it was Slater's name on the screen. Yeah, no one other than Abigail was getting much sleep tonight. Slater hadn't sent a text but was calling instead.

Hell.

This couldn't be good, and he hoped the killer hadn't already launched an attack here at the ranch.

Since Ruston didn't want the sound of Slater's voice waking the baby, he didn't put the call on speaker. "Slater," he whispered. "What's wrong?"

"I just got a report that SAPD found another body," Slater said.

That caused everything inside him to clench. "Is it Allie?" he asked.

"No," Slater was quick to answer.

Even though he hadn't put the call on speaker, Gracelyn obviously heard that, and she made a sharp sound of relief.

"SAPD thinks this one is a suicide. Or at least it was set up to look that way, with a single gunshot wound to the head," Slater explained. "The dead guy is Zimmer."

Chapter Thirteen

Gracelyn sat in the family room at the McCullough ranch, holding Abigail and waiting while Duncan was talking on the phone to Noah about the latest updates in the investigation. She felt drained. Numb. But she knew those feelings would have been much worse had it been her sister's body that was found.

That was what she'd first thought when Slater had called hours earlier to tell them what had happened. Gracelyn had thought that Zimmer had gotten to Allie and had silenced her for good.

Instead, Zimmer was the one who was dead.

Gracelyn had read the preliminary report that Noah had done, and someone out walking their dog had spotted Zimmer slumped behind the wheel of his truck that was parked outside a long-stay motel. As Slater had said, he'd died from a gunshot wound to the head that appeared to be self-inflicted.

She wasn't buying that.

And apparently neither was Ruston, Joelle, Duncan, Slater or Noah. Like her, they were all convinced that Zimmer had been murdered. Probably by the same person who'd already murdered at least three other people and had hired those fake cops to come after Ruston and her.

"You should eat," Ruston said, tipping his head to the

breakfast sandwich that was on the end table to her right. It was one of many sandwiches that Luca had dropped off from the diner.

Ruston leaned in and smiled at Abigail. "Hey, sweet girl." He brushed a kiss on her cheek.

Abigail turned her head toward him, something she'd only recently started doing, and she studied Ruston for a couple of seconds before her tiny mouth bowed into a smile. The baby's attention then shifted to his badge that he had pinned to his shirt. It was shiny, since it was new and had been delivered earlier, courtesy of Captain O'Malley. Gracelyn was glad the captain had made that kind of effort, because it showed she still had plenty of faith in Ruston as a cop.

"Want me to hold Abigail while you eat?" Ruston asked.

Gracelyn wasn't sure her stomach was settled enough to handle any food, but it was obvious Ruston was concerned about her. Added to that, she really did need to try to eat something, since she couldn't even remember when her last meal had been. So, she handed him the baby and picked up the sandwich. Just as Duncan finished his latest phone call.

"Time of death for Zimmer was about ten last night. The medical examiner agrees that it's not suicide," Duncan said right off. "The angle of the shot is off. Good, but off."

"Close range or from a distance?" Joelle asked. She was in the chair next to Duncan and was eating a bagel that had been slathered with cream cheese.

"Close range but not point-blank," Duncan supplied. "Noah believes Zimmer's killer was waiting for him, and when Zimmer parked in front of his motel room, the killer shot him. Not through the glass. Zimmer had apparently lowered his windows."

"Because he knew his killer and was going to talk to him or her?" Ruston wanted to know.

"Maybe. Noah said the AC wasn't working in Zimmer's truck, so both the driver's and passenger's windows were down. He was shot through the passenger's window. The killer could have simply walked up to him, fired and then placed the gun in Zimmer's hand to try to make it look as if he'd pulled the trigger."

Gracelyn took a moment, fixing that scenario in her mind. "Is the gun registered to Zimmer?"

Duncan shook his head. "It was reported stolen about a year ago, so no way to trace it. Zimmer had a slide holster in the back of his jeans, but there was no gun inside it."

"Which meant the killer likely took it," Ruston said, shaking his head. "Was the motel parking lot well lit? And please tell me there are security cameras nearby."

Duncan's sigh said it all. "No cameras, bad lighting, and in a neighborhood where it's rare for someone to come forward and report what they saw."

The killer would have known all of that. Added to that, it'd been night, and the darkness would have given him an advantage.

Duncan washed down a bite of his breakfast burrito with some coffee and shifted his attention to Gracelyn. "There's been no sign of your sister. Why don't you go ahead and leave her another message on the private Facebook page? Tell her I want to talk to her about that deal she was looking to make."

"I will," Gracelyn said, taking out her phone to do that. "But I doubt she'll believe that."

"Probably not, but we need to find her. And, yeah, there's a slim-to-none chance of a deal, but if she cooperates, the DA might show some leniency."

Gracelyn didn't say aloud that Allie didn't deserve leniency. Not after what she'd tried to do to Abigail, but that wasn't for her to decide. Right now, Allie just needed to turn herself in or she would likely end up dead like Zimmer.

She left the message for Allie just as Duncan's phone rang. "It's Hank, one of the ranch hands," he relayed.

Gracelyn couldn't hear what the hand said, but whatever it was caused Duncan to get to his feet and make a beeline toward the front window. "We have a visitor," Duncan explained. "It's Tony. He said he's here to make a confession."

"A confession?" Ruston and she repeated in unison.

Mercy. Gracelyn hadn't seen this coming. Then again, maybe this was just another ruse to get close to Ruston and her so he could kill them.

Duncan must have had the same concerns, because he glanced back at Joelle. "Why don't Slater and you go ahead and take the baby upstairs?"

Joelle nodded, immediately got up and took Abigail from Ruston. Gracelyn figured Duncan was about to tell her to go with them, but he didn't.

"Tony's still at the end of the road, and the hands can and will block him from coming closer. It's up to you whether or not you want to see him," Duncan explained, looking at both Ruston and her. He listened to something else Hank said. "Tony's alone and volunteered to be disarmed before he comes in the house."

Before Duncan had added that last part, Gracelyn had figured they would be having this conversation with Tony on the porch and Ruston and she would be tucked back in the foyer.

"We'll talk to him," Gracelyn agreed after she got a nod from Ruston. "I want to hear what he has to say."

They had a lot of information about the murders and attacks. Info from plenty of sources that might or might not be reliable. Zimmer, Allie, Charla and Devin. If Tony was truly here to confess, then all of those pieces of info might actually fit. They might be able to make an arrest and put a stop to any other murders or attacks.

"Frisk him thoroughly," Duncan told the ranch hand on the phone. "Hold on to any weapons he has and then drive him to the house in your truck. If this is some kind of last-ditch effort, Tony's vehicle could be rigged with explosives."

Gracelyn hadn't even considered that, a reminder that she really needed to try to keep a clear head. If Tony was desperate enough to make a confession, then he might want to first do as much damage as possible.

Since Ruston and Duncan were already at the front windows and had their weapons drawn, Gracelyn moved to the side one and took out her gun as well. The ranch hands were keeping an eye on the yard to make sure no one tried to sneak into the house, but she needed to do something to make sure they weren't attacked.

It was a good five minutes before Gracelyn saw the truck coming up the road, and she lost sight of it when it turned down the driveway toward the house. Both Duncan and Ruston stayed in place until the driver turned off the engine, and then they went to the door.

"Hang back until we have Tony inside," Duncan told her. "I've got to turn off the security system for just a couple of seconds. Once Tony is inside, I'll turn it back on."

Gracelyn muttered an agreement and continued to keep watch out the side window, especially since there'd be that short pause for the security. It wasn't long before the footsteps on the porch had her turning in that direction. Tony stepped in, and while he frowned at Duncan and Ruston basically holding him at gunpoint, he didn't protest.

"I won't take much of your time," Tony insisted, spearing Ruston with his gaze before he did the same to her.

Duncan maneuvered Tony into the foyer so he could shut the door, and Gracelyn saw him rearm the security system. Only then did Gracelyn give Tony her full attention. He looked disheveled, with his clothes wrinkled and stubble that was well past the fashionable stage. Like the rest of them, Tony didn't appear to have gotten much sleep.

"I'm resigning from SAPD today," Tony stated. He'd somehow managed to keep the emotion out of his flat tone, but the emotion was there in his eyes. A mix of anger and frustration. And guilt.

"You said you were here to make a confession," Ruston pressed. No flat tone for him. There was a "get on with this" edge to his voice.

Tony nodded. "Internal Affairs is examining my financials, and it won't take them long to discover that I accepted money from Marty. Payment in exchange for redirecting investigations so they didn't lead to him."

Ruston uttered a single raw word of profanity. "You sold out Gracelyn and me at the baby farm?"

"No," Tony was quick to say. "Hell, no. Nothing like that." He groaned and shook his head. "I was broke and behind in my child support. My ex was going to report me, and I would have maybe ended up losing my job, so I borrowed money from Marty. I know it was stupid," he quickly added, "but I was desperate."

"Desperate enough to sell out your badge," Ruston snapped, taking the words right out of Gracelyn's mouth.

Tony sighed. "Yes, but I didn't see it as selling out. I thought, stupidly thought," he amended, "that I could get my ex off my

back and find another way to pay Marty what I owed him."
He paused. "But Marty didn't want payback in the form of
money. He wanted a cop in his pocket. He got one, but I never
compromised the safety of any officers. Like I said, I only re-
directed investigations away from Marty."

The anger and disgust rolled through her, and Gracelyn
had to tamp some of that down before she could speak. "Did
you tell Internal Affairs this?"

"No, but I will. I wanted to tell Ruston and you first, and
then I'll talk to Charla. Then I'll turn myself in."

"Charla doesn't know what you've done?" Gracelyn
asked.

"No, and she'll be crushed," Tony concluded.

Maybe. But if Charla was the killer, then she might be
pleased about this development, because in a way, it took
some of the focus off the person behind the attacks and
murders.

Tony pulled in a long breath. "I didn't directly do anything to put the two of you in danger, but by protecting
Marty, the danger happened anyway."

Yes, it had. And Internal Affairs would no doubt question him about that once he told them what he'd done.

If he told them, that was.

It occurred to her that Tony might be planning to go on
the run. But if so, why come here first? Was this actually
some kind of ploy to distract them? That thought flashed
in her head just as Duncan's phone rang.

"It's Hank," Duncan muttered, keeping his gaze on Tony
while he took the call. Gracelyn couldn't hear what the hand
said, but whatever it was prompted Duncan to mutter his
own word of profanity, and he shook his head. "No, search
them and bring them up. I'll call for every available deputy
to respond." And Duncan proceeded to contact Dispatch.

Gracelyn's stomach dropped. "Are we about to be attacked?" she asked Duncan the second he finished the call.

"I don't think so. Hank said that Devin just arrived," Duncan explained. "And he has Allie with him. Devin wants me to arrest her."

"Allie," Gracelyn murmured, and she looked at Ruston to get his take on this.

He was apparently on the same wavelength, because she could see the uneasiness in his eyes. Then again, that feeling had already been there for both of them with Tony's arrival. Now it was skyrocketing.

It could be a coincidence that two of their suspects, Tony and Devin, were there at the same time, but Gracelyn didn't like coincidences. Maybe Tony and Devin were working together. This could be the start of another attack.

Part of her was relieved her sister was alive. But there was no relief whatsoever in the fact that Devin was the one bringing her in. Well, supposedly he was, anyway. Gracelyn didn't trust Devin any more than she did Tony or her sister.

Or Charla.

Since Charla was the only one of their suspects who hadn't shown up, that made Gracelyn wonder where she was. Was she standing back, watching this all play out after she'd set it in motion?

Perhaps.

Or Devin could be the one playing games here. But if he was the one responsible for the murders and attacks, then why hadn't he just killed Allie? That didn't help settle Gracelyn's worries about Devin, since this could be a sort of reverse psychology. A way to try to make himself look innocent by keeping one loose end alive.

"I don't want Allie in the house," Ruston insisted. "She might try to go after Abigail."

Gracelyn was in complete agreement, and apparently so was Duncan since he didn't protest that. "Hank, let me speak to Devin," Duncan told the ranch hand. "I'm putting the call on speaker."

The downside to that was Tony was standing right there and would be able to hear everything, but that was better than the alternative of bringing Devin and Allie to the house. Or sending Tony on his way. If Tony had hooked up with Devin to do another attack, Gracelyn thought it would be best if they weren't together. Then again, it was possible Devin was counting on Tony to be his inside man in whatever might be about to happen. That was why Gracelyn kept her attention pinned to Tony.

"Don't," she warned Tony when he reached for something in his pocket.

Tony huffed, clearly annoyed at her warning. "I just want to call SAPD and get you some help out here."

"No calls," Duncan ordered, muting his phone so that Devin wouldn't be able to hear any of this. "Just stand there and don't say anything."

Tony's eyes narrowed, but he held up his hands as if in mock surrender. Oh, yes. Gracelyn was definitely going to watch him.

Duncan's phone began to ding with a series of texts, and Gracelyn caught glimpses of his screen. Carmen, Luca and Woodrow were on their way.

"Sheriff Holder," Devin said the moment he was on the phone. "I've got Allie with me."

"So I heard. How did you know I was here?" Duncan asked.

Devin seemed to hesitate as if he hadn't expected the question. "Allie told me about the shooting at the sheriff's office, and I figured the place was a giant crime scene right now."

It was, and since the CSIs were working the scene, the building was temporarily closed, and Duncan and the other deputies were working from home.

"I guessed you'd come back here with Gracelyn," Devin tacked on to his explanation.

"And you decided to bring Allie with you." The remark was heavy with skepticism.

"He brought me here against my will," Allie shouted. "He tied my hands and kidnapped me."

"I found her trying to sneak into my house," Devin countered. "I'd changed the locks, and she'd broken a window. When I confronted her, she tried to punch me. Then bite me. Then scratch me." He sounded riled about that. "I brought her here so you can arrest her."

"SAPD could have done that much faster," Duncan was quick to point out.

More silence from Devin. But not from Allie. She continued to curse and yell, and Gracelyn hoped she didn't break out of whatever restraints were on her.

"I thought you'd want to handle the arrest," Devin finally said. "SAPD might not turn her over to you to answer for what she did, and I know Gracelyn especially will want her sister punished."

"Abigail is mine." That came as another shout from Allie. "I can do with her what I want."

The words hit Gracelyn like a heavyweight's fists. Allie could be just ranting out of rage, but that sounded very much like the threat that it was. If Allie got her hands on Abigail, there was no telling what she'd do to the child.

Duncan sighed and scrubbed his hand over his face, and he checked the text messages that were lighting up his

Protecting the Newborn

phone. "Stay put at the end of the road. Deputies Vanetti and Leonard will be there in just a few minutes. They can take custody of Allie and transport her to the county jail."

That brought out even louder shouts and cursing from Allie. "Gracelyn?" her sister called out. "I know you're there. Help me. Help your sister. Please," Allie begged. "Stop the deputies from taking me."

Gracelyn nearly spoke, not to give Allie any assurance she would stop the deputies, though. But to tell Allie that she would arrange for a lawyer to represent her.

"Gracelyn," Allie went on, and this time she spoke her name as if coated with venom. "So much for sisterly love, huh? You won't even help me. Well, to hell with you, Gracelyn. I wish the gunmen would have killed you. I wish you were dead." She was shrieking by the time she got out those last words.

Gracelyn wanted to be immune to them. But she wasn't. The words and her sister's hatred sliced her to the bone.

"Hell, Allie managed to get out of the car," Devin snarled.

Through the phone, Gracelyn heard Devin shouting her sister's name just as there was the squeal of brakes.

And the deadly-sounding thud that followed.

Chapter Fourteen

Ruston finished his latest phone call, this one an update from Slater. A call he purposely hadn't put on speaker since Gracelyn was talking with one of the ER nurses, Eileen Parsons, and he hadn't wanted Eileen to hear anything that might then end up as gossip. Added to that, if Slater had doled out some bad news, Ruston had wanted the chance to soften that news before passing it along to Gracelyn.

Gracelyn didn't look on the verge of falling apart, but he didn't want to add anything else to this already bad situation. Allie was now out of nearly seven hours of surgery, but she was critical. The surgeon had already told Gracelyn and him that Allie's chances of survival weren't good.

Ruston hadn't actually seen Allie since she'd bolted into the road and been hit by a rancher who just happened to be driving by at the time. But he'd heard the sound of the impact. He'd heard the urgency in Hank's voice, too, when he'd shouted for Devin to call an ambulance.

And Ruston had seen the blood on the road.

Gracelyn had seen it as well. No way to avoid it since Duncan, Ruston and she had left the ranch in a cruiser to come to the hospital, and they'd had to drive right past the spot where Allie had been hit.

Ruston had dreaded that drive for a lot of reasons, but

it hadn't been optional. Not after the hospital had called Gracelyn to ask her to come in and donate the rare AB negative blood that Allie and she shared. Gracelyn had done that, and now, ten hours later, they were waiting to see if it would save her sister's life.

Even though Allie's last words to Gracelyn had been to wish her dead, Gracelyn clearly didn't feel the same way about Allie. No way was she pleased with pretty much anything Allie had done, but Ruston understood her need to be here. Her need to do whatever she could to keep Allie alive.

Later, if Allie made it, she'd have to answer for the horrible crimes she'd committed. But *later* would have to wait.

Eileen looked over at him when Ruston put his phone away and made his way back toward Gracelyn and her. Not that he had gone far. For one thing, he wouldn't have let Gracelyn out of his sight, and for another, this particular waiting room was small, not much larger than a normal-sized kitchen.

Not many places to have a private conversation.

It was at the other end of the hospital from the much larger ER waiting room, which not only had way too many windows for Ruston's liking but also multiple points of entry. That was why Duncan and he had insisted on using this area, which had been set up for families to wait for surgical patients. No windows. Only one way in and out, and Duncan was guarding that.

Literally.

Duncan was pacing up and down the hall in front of the open archway entrance while he was on the phone, dealing with all the various moving parts of multiple investigations. That included making sure the hospital itself was secure.

Duncan had brought in reserve deputies for that as well, but there was always the concern that someone could slip in.

Or had already slipped in.

There had been well over a two-hour gap between the time that Gracelyn had gotten the call to ask if she'd donate blood and their arrival here at the hospital. There'd been no reserve deputies on the doors during that gap, so someone could have gotten in then.

"Any news about Allie?" Ruston asked Eileen.

The nurse had come in just as Ruston had gotten the call from Slater, so he hadn't heard anything of what she'd come to tell Gracelyn. But Ruston figured Eileen wasn't there to deliver the news that Allie was dead. That would almost certainly come from a doctor.

Eileen nodded. "They had to take her back into surgery to try to stop some internal bleeding. We're not sure how long the procedure will take." She sighed, checked her watch. "You guys have been here a long time, and I just wanted to check on the two of you and see if you needed anything."

Yeah, he needed a safe place for Gracelyn. Safer than here, anyway. But that wasn't something Eileen could fix.

Ruston looked at Gracelyn to see if she intended to take Eileen up on her offer, but she shook her head. "We're fine for now, but thanks," Ruston told the nurse, and he went to Gracelyn to pull her into his arms.

"What did Slater tell you?" she immediately asked. "Is Abigail all right?"

"She's fine. All the security measures are still in place."

All was a lot. Joelle, Slater and Luca were inside the locked-down ranch house with Abigail, and Slater had brought in his ranch hands to patrol the grounds with the other hands already keeping watch. A reserve deputy was at the end of the road to stop anyone from driving up to the house.

That included Tony or Devin. Ruston hadn't wanted them hanging around, so he'd sent them both on their way, though Devin would have to come in and give a statement about why he'd brought Allie to the ranch in the first place. But that would have to wait.

Part of Ruston had wanted to haul Devin in if only so he could keep him under a careful watch for a while, but the deputies and Duncan were already stretched thin. Added to that, the sheriff's office was still shut down, and with Duncan on guard duty, it would have meant bringing Devin to the hospital. Since that wouldn't have pleased anyone, Duncan had sent Devin home.

Hopefully that wouldn't turn out to be a fatal mistake.

"Slater said no one has gotten onto the ranch," Ruston emphasized before he told her the rest. "But one of the hands did see a vehicle driving slowly on the road that leads to the turnoff to the ranch. He didn't recognize the car, so he got the license plate and phoned Slater. When Slater ran it, he learned the vehicle belongs to Charla."

Gracelyn huffed. "What was she doing there?"

"I'm not sure. And it might not have been her behind the wheel. The hand thought the driver was a man."

"A hired gun?" But she immediately dismissed that with a head shake. "No, Charla wouldn't have let a hired gun use her car."

"Probably not," he agreed. "If she's not behind the attacks, someone could have stolen her car to make it look as if she was in the area."

He thought of another possibility, though. That Charla had hoped this mystery driver would be mistaken for her and therefore give her some kind of alibi.

"Slater did try to call her," Ruston added, "but it went straight to voicemail, so he left a message for Charla to contact either him or me."

Whether or not Charla would call back was anyone's guess. Ditto for her revealing what she was actually doing there. She could have been setting up another attack. Or she could have simply been looking for Tony. Ruston had no idea where he was. Then again, he could say that about all of their suspects except for Allie.

"You're thinking how vulnerable we are here at the hospital," Gracelyn muttered, and when he pulled himself out of his own thoughts, he realized she was staring up at him.

Ruston nodded. "Vulnerable here and anywhere else we happen to go," he admitted.

Gracelyn matched his nod. "Once Allie's out of surgery and we're back at the ranch, we should talk about that plan for us as bait. And, no, I don't like it any more than you do," she was quick to add. "But the truth is, we're no closer to catching this killer than we were two days ago. You and I are what he or she wants. We're what could cause the killer to slip up and get caught."

Every word of that was true, but it didn't minimize the risks they'd be taking. That was why he tried again to offer her a plan B. "I can be the bait, and you can be part of the security setup. You can be the one to help pen in the killer."

Ruston could tell from the look in her eyes that she was going to argue with that. She didn't want to be tucked away somewhere while he was basically dealing with a serial killer. But she didn't get a chance to voice that because of the sound of footsteps.

Both Gracelyn and he put their hands over their guns, proof of just how on edge they were, but it was Duncan who stepped into the doorway.

"Anything on Allie?" he immediately asked.

"She's back in surgery," Gracelyn answered. "Internal bleeding. It doesn't sound good."

Duncan muttered an "I'm sorry" and then paused. "The medical examiner found something on Zimmer's body."

That got their attention, and they pinned their gazes on Duncan.

"Zimmer had homemade tats between his toes," Duncan explained. "Recent ones. It appears to be a username and password. For what, we don't know, but I just got off the phone with the tech guys who are going to try to find out what they could mean."

Ruston thought back through all the things Zimmer had told Gracelyn and him in that phone conversation. "If Zimmer wasn't lying about investigating the baby farm, this could be his notes or something. Heck, it could give us the name of the killer."

"Yeah," Duncan muttered, not sounding overly hopeful, yet there was some hope there. Maybe because they didn't have any other leads.

"Did Slater tell you about Charla's vehicle being spotted near the ranch?" Ruston asked him.

"He did," Duncan verified. "Any chance your pal Noah Ryland can locate her and ask her about that?"

"I'll check," Ruston said, taking out his phone. "While I'm at it, I'll see if he can get any feed from security cameras near Devin's. It'd be interesting to see if his story about Allie trying to break in meshes with what shows up on the cameras."

Ruston started the text but then glanced up when the lights flickered. He frowned because there wasn't a storm to cause any interference. Frowned, too, because any and everything that wasn't normal was suspicious.

His suspicions skyrocketed.

The lights went out, and the room was plunged into total darkness.

GRACELYN HEARD HERSELF GASP, and she thought maybe her heart had skipped a beat or two. She immediately fumbled for her phone, but before she could take it out, a light came on. Not the overhead ones. This was a much dimmer one that was fixed on the wall.

"The generator kicked in," she heard Ruston say.

Obviously, he didn't think the loss of power was a fluke, because he'd stepped into the doorway next to Duncan and had already drawn his gun. Duncan and she did the same.

And they waited.

Her heartbeat started to race and thud as she thought of all the things that could go wrong. The killer could be coming after them. Right now. He could be using the dim lights as a way to get closer. But Ruston, Duncan and she were ready for that.

She hoped.

Gracelyn prayed the killer hadn't come up with a way to get to them that they couldn't stop. Or a way to crush her without even being near her.

"Abigail," she muttered, and the fear came, soaring.

Because if the killer had arranged for this, there could be an attack at the ranch. Her hands were far from being steady when she took out her phone and made a call to Joelle.

More waiting. Each fraction of a second seemed to take an eternity, but Joelle finally answered.

"Is everything okay?" Joelle and Gracelyn blurted out at the same time.

Apparently, Joelle was just as much on edge as she was. "The power went out at the hospital," Gracelyn explained. "We're okay, though," she quickly added when Duncan shot her a pleading glance. He obviously didn't want his pregnant wife to worry about him. "I just wanted to make sure everything was all right there."

"We're okay here, too," Joelle assured her. "No power outages. No signs of anyone trying to get near the house. Abigail just had a bottle and is asleep." She paused a moment. "Is Allie out of surgery?"

"Not yet."

"Okay, keep me posted," Joelle said, and she paused again. "You think the killer messed with the power, don't you?"

Gracelyn considered lying, but Joelle was a cop and would likely see right through that. "It's something we're considering. But the three of us are together, and we'll stay that way to give each other plenty of backup."

"All right." Joelle's voice was more than a little shaky now. "Just be careful, and tell Duncan I love him. Wait, don't do that," she quickly amended. "Because that sounds like a goodbye. Tell him to come home when he can."

"I will," Gracelyn assured her. She ended the call and relayed the message. "Joelle says to come home when you can."

Duncan made a sound of agreement, but heaven knew when that would be. For the moment, though, they weren't going anywhere. If the killer was indeed in the building, then it was best to stay put and have him or her come to them. Three against one. Well, three against an army, if the killer had backup.

But Gracelyn had to pray that wouldn't happen.

Duncan was looking to the left of the hall while Ruston was keeping an eye on the right. Gracelyn was between them and volleyed glances in both directions and at a stained glass window high on the wall across from them. She seriously doubted it would open, but it was possible someone could shoot their way through it. If that happened, she'd have a fairly good shot to stop anyone coming in that way.

A phone rang, the sound slicing through the silence, and Gracelyn saw the screen of Duncan's cell light up. "It's Anita Denny," he said, referring to one of the reserve deputies he'd posted around the hospital.

Duncan answered it, sandwiching the phone between his ear and shoulder while he continued to keep watch in the hall. He hadn't put the call on speaker, probably because he didn't want the sound of the deputy's voice to interfere with the sound of any approaching footsteps. That, and he likely didn't want Anita to give away anything that might help a killer pinpoint their location.

"Are you okay?" Duncan asked, and there was plenty of alarm in his voice.

Oh, mercy. Something had happened.

"Describe him," Duncan insisted a moment later, and then he paused, no doubt to listen to what Anita was telling him. "And you're sure it was a man?" Another pause, followed by some muttered profanity. "All right. Stay put, and I'll get someone to you," he said, ending the call.

"Who do you need me to call or text?" Ruston immediately wanted to know.

"Text Woodrow," Duncan was quick to say. "He's with the medical examiner and can be here in about fifteen minutes. I want him to go to the east side of the hospital to check on Anita. She says she's okay, but I'm not convinced."

"What happened to her?" Ruston asked Duncan while he sent the message to Woodrow.

"Someone tossed some rocks from the roof of the hospital. A few of them hit her, and when Anita looked up, she saw a man looming over the side. Just the top of his head, though, not his actual face. Anita called out to him, but he disappeared from sight."

So, it could be either Devin or Tony. Or someone that Charla had hired.

Or none of the above.

Gracelyn wanted to believe this was some kind of prank. But it didn't feel like one at all.

"Who can I call to get someone onto the roof?" Gracelyn wanted to know.

"Anita's already done it," Duncan explained. "Two hospital security guards are headed up there now. I'm contacting Dispatch to see who they can get up there to help them."

Gracelyn had no idea if the guards could handle something like confronting a killer, but she suspected the confrontation wouldn't happen. The killer wanted Ruston and her, not the guards. So, maybe this was some kind of distraction? Certainly, the killer wasn't hoping to lure them up to the roof, too?

But maybe that would work.

Partially, anyway.

If the killer managed to hold the security guards hostage, Duncan might go up there. Might. And that would leave Ruston and her alone. But even then, they certainly weren't defenseless.

Duncan had just made his call to the dispatcher when Gracelyn heard something that had them all stopping cold.

A gasp.

It had come from the direction of the nurses' station just up the hall, and they all turned in that direction, each of them bringing up their guns. The light was dim in that area, too, but not so dim that Gracelyn didn't see the nurse lying face down on the floor. For a horrifying moment, Gracelyn thought she was dead, but the woman lifted her head and then tried to scramble away from something.

Or rather someone.

There, in the shadows, Gracelyn saw a figure wearing all black who was crouched down behind the nurse. Gracelyn couldn't see his face. Heck, couldn't even tell if it was a man.

Like Ruston and Duncan, Gracelyn took aim at him, but none of them had a clean shot because the person grabbed the nurse, hooked an arm around her neck and used her as a shield. That was when Gracelyn realized why she couldn't see the person's face.

Because there was a gas mask covering it.

A split second later, there was the thudding sound of something hitting the floor. A small canister, and white smoke immediately spewed from it. One whiff, though, and Gracelyn knew it wasn't smoke.

It was tear gas.

Her eyes started to burn like fire, and she began to cough. She tried to bat the gas away from her face but couldn't. It was everywhere, engulfing them in the thick cloud, and it was having the same effect on Ruston and Duncan, too, because they were coughing as well.

Not the killer, though.

That thought was loud and clear in her head. The killer had on that mask, which meant he could walk right through the gas and get to them.

Gracelyn tried to run. Tried to get to some fresh air so she'd have enough breath to fight back. To protect anyone who was now in this killer's path. But the coughing overtook everything, and she couldn't see. She had no choice but to drop to her knees.

Gracelyn felt someone take hold of her arm. Not a gentle grip. A hard, wrenching one that dragged her to her feet and ripped the gun from her hand.

"Move," the voice snarled.

The person's crushing grip made sure she did that. Moving her away from the waiting room. And toward the exit. That was when Gracelyn realized what was happening.

She was being kidnapped.

Chapter Fifteen

With his pulse racing and adrenaline firing on all cylinders, Ruston could hear the sounds around him. Footsteps, coughing, gasps for breath. He was doing plenty of coughing and gasping of his own, and he was on his knees. He couldn't see anything but the ghost-white tear gas.

He couldn't see the person who'd set off the canister.

Ruston figured the guy was there, though, and had done this so he could kill Gracelyn and him. The tear gas would make that easier for him to do that since he was wearing a mask, but first he'd have to get to them, and Ruston needed to do something to prevent that from happening.

Hard to do anything when his throat and lungs were on fire, and the coughing was making it impossible to do much of anything. He tried to call out to Gracelyn, to tell her to stay right next to him. However, he failed. Everything inside him was yelling for him to get away, to breathe in some fresh air. But he also needed to protect Gracelyn, and at the moment, he clearly couldn't do that.

Ruston wasn't even sure where she was.

He tried to move. Tried to listen. And he could hear more of the shuffling of footsteps mixed in with the other sounds. What he couldn't hear was Gracelyn or Duncan.

Along with essentially blinding him and sending him

into a coughing fit, Ruston was disoriented and couldn't tell exactly where he was. He kept his gun gripped in his right hand and reached out with his left. He felt what he thought was the hall wall and not the archway opening of the waiting room. If so, that meant Gracelyn was probably behind him.

He staggered in what he hoped was the right direction to find her, and he'd made it a few steps when he heard a door open. That was followed by a rush of light and the fresh air that his lungs were screaming for. It cleared out some of the gas mist, but his vision was still plenty blurry.

But not his mind.

The thoughts were racing through him. One bad thought in particular. If someone had opened a door to the outside, then it could mean the tear-gas thug was escaping. Not alone, though. He could have Gracelyn with him.

"Gracelyn?" he tried to call out and managed it despite the coughing.

No answer.

He wanted to believe that was because her throat didn't allow her to respond, but his gut told him it was something much worse.

Ruston gathered up every bit of his strength and got to his feet so he could get to that open door. He made it there one staggering step at a time, and he hoped Duncan was doing the same. Someone was moving in his direction, anyway. If it was the killer, then he'd no doubt have a clean shot.

But no gunshots came.

"Where's Gracelyn?" he heard Duncan ask through the strangling coughs.

That gave Ruston another jolt of adrenaline that fueled him to move even faster to the door. He stepped out, the fresh night air engulfing him, and he nearly tripped over something. No, not something.

Someone.

For a horrifying moment, he thought the person on the ground was Gracelyn, but it wasn't. It was Nelda Martin, one of the deputies guarding the doors. She was in a crumpled heap, and there was blood on her head.

Cursing, Ruston stooped down to check for a pulse while he frantically scanned the parking lot that was just on the other side of a grassy area. There were some vehicles, including a Saddle Ridge cruiser that Nelda had likely used to come to the hospital, but there was no sign of Gracelyn.

"Hell," Duncan snarled when he stepped outside. "Is Nelda alive?"

Ruston nodded. "She's got a pulse." He kept looking. Kept listening. And he finally heard something. The sound of an engine being revved. A few seconds later, he saw the black SUV speeding out of the parking lot. He caught a glimpse of the driver.

Someone in a gas mask.

And he saw Gracelyn. Just for a second.

His heart dropped.

Because, like Nelda, she was unconscious and there was blood on her head.

"Gracelyn!" he called out, running into the parking lot.

"She's in that SUV?" Duncan asked.

"Yeah," Ruston managed, and he tried to tamp down the panic that was crawling through him.

"Use the cruiser," Duncan insisted. He rummaged through Nelda's pocket, came up with the keys and tossed them to Ruston. "Go. I'll be right behind you as soon as I get her some help. I can use one of the other cruisers to track you."

Ruston caught the keys and didn't waste a second. He

ran straight to the cruiser, jumped in and started driving. Fast. As if Gracelyn's life depended on it.

Which it did.

He practically flew out of the parking lot, and some of the tightness in his chest eased up just a little when he spotted the SUV. Again, it was just a glimpse before it disappeared around a curve. But at least Ruston knew what direction it was going.

Out of town.

Well, maybe. A sickening thought occurred to him, that maybe there was more than one SUV, that the one he saw was meant to lead him in the wrong direction. That was possible, but since he didn't have a lot of options, he went after it. He had to get to Gracelyn and stop her from being killed.

The image of the blood on her head flashed in his mind, but he had to shove that aside. That would only tear apart his focus, and right now, he needed all the focus he could get. He had to catch up with that SUV.

The plates on the SUV were almost certainly bogus, so Ruston knew he wouldn't be able to rely on that even if he got the license numbers. He had to keep the vehicle in sight and follow it to wherever they were taking Gracelyn.

And that gave him another flood of thoughts.

Gracelyn must have been alive if the driver had taken her. If he'd already killed her, he would have just left her in the hospital. So, this was a kidnapping.

Why?

Again, that brought some bad thoughts. Maybe to use Gracelyn to lure him out? But why not just take him along with her?

Ruston thought back to what had gone on in the hall of the hospital. He'd only seen one person, so it was possible the kidnapper couldn't get both of them out. Even if he'd managed to hold both Gracelyn and him at gunpoint, it would have been difficult to get them out of the hospital and into the SUV. Gracelyn and he would have fought back.

The image of the blood flashed again.

She likely had fought back. And the thug who had her had hurt her. Had probably knocked her unconscious. Or drugged her. Either way, when she came to, she'd try to escape. The kidnapper wouldn't just let that happen, which meant Gracelyn could end up being killed in the fight. That was why Ruston had to keep the SUV in sight. It was the only way he had now of getting to Gracelyn.

The SUV sped out of town, and the driver must have had the accelerator floored, because Ruston wasn't gaining on him. Thankfully, he wasn't losing either. The SUV stayed ahead, tearing across the rural road, and so far there were no other vehicles around. But the road wasn't straight either. There were plenty of curves just ahead. Since the driver might not be familiar with that, Ruston hoped he didn't lose control and crash.

Ruston had to hit his brakes when he got to the first of that series of curves, but once he was through it, he immediately sped up again. Keeping the SUV in sight.

He cursed when his phone rang because it took some effort to get it out of his pocket while keeping the cruiser from going off the road. Duncan's name was on the screen.

"I'm in a cruiser and am tracking your location," Duncan said the moment Ruston answered it on speaker. "You're heading toward the interstate."

"Yeah," Ruston verified. And that wasn't good. It'd be much harder to follow the SUV once it was in traffic.

Ruston didn't add more to that because he had to fight to keep control through another of those curves. Then he cursed when he was through it and saw the SUV. Not on the road but rather turning off onto what appeared to be a ranch trail. That could mean Gracelyn had regained consciousness and was now fighting her captor. Or this could have been the plan all along, for the captor to meet up with someone else.

Ruston followed.

"Keep tracking me," Ruston told Duncan, and he ended the call so he could focus on his driving.

The cruiser bounced over the uneven rock-and-dirt surface. Ahead of him, the SUV did, too. Then it stopped, and Ruston saw the driver bolt from the SUV and break into a run through the woods.

Ruston braked, bolted from the cruiser and began to run, too. Not toward the driver but to check on Gracelyn. Once he was sure she was all right, then he could go in pursuit.

He hurried to the passenger's-side door.

And his heart went straight to the ground.

Because she wasn't there. No one was. The SUV was empty.

He didn't see any blood, and he certainly hadn't seen her with the escaping driver, but he fired glances all around in case the thug had tossed her out of the vehicle.

Still, nothing.

Ruston tried to tamp down his fear and kept searching. His heartbeat was drumming in his ears now. He was breathing way too fast. But he still heard a ringing sound. Not his phone. He followed the sound to the driver's seat of the SUV, where a cheap-looking cell was ringing. A burner, no doubt.

He didn't have any evidence gloves on him, and it was a risk to touch the phone and contaminate any possible evidence. Still, he knew this call had to do with Gracelyn, so he went ahead and answered it.

"You can save her," the mechanical voice immediately said. "No other cops. Just you, Ruston. If you want to save her, you'll come alone."

He had to get his throat unclamped before he could speak. "Where? Where are you taking her?"

"To the baby farm. Get there fast," the voice warned him before the call ended.

GRACELYN FOUGHT HER way out of the dream. A nightmare. With images of blood and the sound of gunfire. The crushing sensation in her chest of not being able to breathe.

She forced her eyes open, slowly. She had no choice about that. Her head was throbbing, the pain pulsing through her, and she didn't want to make any sudden moves. So, she just sat there, glanced around and listened.

She was in a vehicle, belted into the front seat, and her hands were cuffed together at the wrists. That sent a jolt of panic through her, but she tried not to cry out. She didn't want to make a sound until she had figured out where she was and who had taken her.

The images and memories were all tangled up in her head. Everything swirling. And the pain. Mercy, the pain was still there, too. So, that was why it took long moments for her to latch on to anything. Then it all came together.

And she suddenly remembered what had happened.

The tear gas at the hospital. Being dragged out by a man wearing a mask. Once they were outside, she'd seen the injured deputy on the ground, and she'd managed to break away from her attacker. She ran. For only a second or two, though, before he'd grabbed her by the hair and then slammed her onto the ground.

She'd felt the sharp stab of pain in nearly every part of her body. Then she had fallen and hit her head. After that, everything went dark. Until now. Until she'd woken up in this vehicle. But where was she?

That question quickly faded when another, more important one flashed in her mind.

Where was Ruston?

Was he hurt? Or worse? And what about Duncan? Gracelyn was almost certain they'd still been in the hospital when she had been taken.

She moved her wrists a little, testing out the restraints. Flex-cuffs. It was what cops used to restrain perps. But it was also what Devin had used on Allie.

Allie.

Her thoughts went there for a moment. She wasn't sure how much time had passed since she'd been dragged away from the hospital, but Allie had still been in surgery then. Had been critical. Would the killer send someone after her, too?

Maybe.

But Gracelyn had to hope that the medical staff and the deputies would be able to stop that. Even if they couldn't, she couldn't help Allie herself. Not from here. She'd have to escape to do that.

"You awake?" the driver said.

It was a man. She didn't know who he was, but she thought it was the same person who'd barked out that order for her to move at the hospital.

"Who are you?" she asked, and she tried to make that sound like a demand. It didn't.

Her throat was still burning from the effects of the tear gas, and her vision wasn't 100 percent either. Everything was swimming in and out of focus, but she could see that the man was still wearing a gas mask that concealed all of his face. That blurred vision wasn't helping any with her figuring out where they were either. A country road… somewhere.

"My name's not important," he said, his voice a low, rasping growl. "Just consider me a lackey. A well-paid one," he added with a chuckle. The laughter turned her stomach.

"A lackey," she repeated. So, not the killer. Well, maybe not. She didn't think it was either Devin or Tony, anyway, but the killer could turn out to be someone who wasn't even on their radar. "Where are you taking me? And where's Ruston?"

"Ruston's on a wild-goose chase." He chuckled again.

Oh, that didn't help the panic building inside her. If he was telling the truth, Ruston wasn't coming for her. That could be good, she supposed, since she was probably going to become bait. That was the only reason she could think of as to why she was still alive.

"Why didn't you just take Ruston when you took me?" she asked.

"Too risky to have you both together. My orders were to get you, and once I drop you off, then I can wait around for your boyfriend to show up."

Her bait theory was right. She didn't ask why the lackey was so certain Ruston would come for her. No need. Because Ruston *would* come, and she knew there was nothing she could do or say to stop him. That meant she had to try to end this before Ruston walked into a trap.

But what exactly was this?

Gracelyn sat up in the seat and stared out the windshield at the scenery. Oh, God. She knew where he was taking her. Back to a nightmare.

Back to the baby farm.

"Now, don't go hyperventilating on me," the man said as if it was part of his continuing joke. "Before I drop you off, I'm to give you a message. My boss knows the medical examiner found the username and password for an online storage site that Zimmer set up. If you give it to him, he won't gun down Ruston."

So, that was what the killer wanted. Zimmer had hidden away something that could ID the killer.

"I don't know that information," she said.

"Then you'll get it." He pressed the phone function on his dash screen, and she saw Ruston's name and number pop up. "Tell Ruston what you need and ask him to bring it to you."

He didn't give her a chance to respond or even gather her breath. He just pressed the number, and Ruston immediately answered.

"Who is this?" he demanded. "Do you have Gracelyn?"

"I do indeed have your little darlin'," the man verified, "and this is how you'll get her back. Tell him, Gracelyn. Spell it out for him."

"Ruston," she managed to say. She wished she sounded stronger. Because she was. Despite the nightmare bubbling up inside her, she was a heck of a lot stronger than she sounded.

Think, she told herself. Ruston would be just as frantic as she was, so she had to be smart about what she said.

"I'm okay," she told Ruston and hoped he believed that. If he thought she'd been injured, that might cloud his judgment. He might be willing to do anything to get to her.

"Where are you?" he asked, and yes, there was a sharp intensity in his voice.

"Apparently, on the way to the baby farm."

Ruston cursed, and she heard the sound of a vehicle engine. He was coming for her.

"The lackey who took me didn't tell me the name of his boss, but the killer wants the username and password of Zimmer's accounts," she explained. "The ones he tatted on the inside of his wrist."

Gracelyn had purposely added that last bit of wrong information to confirm to Ruston something he no doubt already knew. That if he showed up at the baby farm, it'd be a trap to kill them both. Once the killer had the username and code, then he'd have no use for Ruston and her.

"Now, here's the deal, Ruston," the lackey said. "You gotta come alone and you gotta bring that username and password. Understand?"

"Yeah," Ruston said, his voice flat and cold. "If you hurt Gracelyn, I'll kill you. Understand?"

The lackey chuckled. "We'll see about that when you get here. Hurry, and if you're not alone, then Gracelyn dies on the spot."

With that, he ended the call and turned onto a familiar road. She had memorized this road and the surrounding area before Ruston and she had gone in undercover. It hadn't changed in a year. The trees that lined the narrow road seemed just as menacing. So did the building that sat just ahead. Not an actual house, but a compound that had once been owned by militia members. It was a mishmash of structures that had been cobbled together. Some parts freight containers, other parts prefab houses, all joined together by what she knew were mazelike halls.

There were no lights on that she could see. No obvious security either. The place looked deserted.

But she was betting it wasn't.

No. There was likely at least one person inside, waiting for her. Waiting for Ruston, too. And she wondered if it was Devin, Charla or Tony.

This would be a way to tie up many loose ends if the killer managed to get access to Zimmer's files and eliminate Ruston and her. But why was the killer so sure that Ruston and she had anything that would incriminate him?

One answer came to mind.

Because the killer knew they wouldn't stop until they got to the truth. They would hunt until they had eliminated the threat to Abigail. Any one of their suspects would know that, too.

The gravel crunched between the tires of the SUV as the driver pulled to a stop. "Man, oh, man, this mask is hot. Sweatin' up a storm underneath."

"You can take it off," she challenged.

He laughed again, that low chuckle that made her want to punch him. This wasn't a joke. This was her life. Hers and Ruston's, and this snake was playing a huge part in putting them in danger.

"Now, now," he scolded. "You don't want to see my face because then I would have to kill you. If you're gonna die, it won't be by my hands."

"No, you'll just turn me over to a killer and pretend the only thing you did wrong was take money to bring me here." This time, she was pleased with her tone. Anger. So much anger. She was channeling every bit of what was churning inside her. "Is that what you plan on telling yourself to help you sleep at night?"

"I sleep just fine," he snarled. He got out and began walking to the passenger's-side door to open it.

Gracelyn got ready. Well, as ready as she could, considering her hands were cuffed. No way to get out of that, and even though she fumbled with the seat belt, she couldn't unlatch it. So, she turned her body and tried to get into a position to do some damage.

The man opened the door, and he leaned in to unbuckle her seat belt. She smelled the sweat on him and could see that the moisture had built up behind the eye coverings of the gas mask. She hoped that meant he also had limited vision.

And that he wouldn't see the attack coming.

The moment he stepped back to pull her out of the SUV, she swung her legs around and kicked him. She aimed for his throat. Missed. But managed to land a kicking blow into his chest.

Cursing, he staggered back, but before he could get out of the way, she kicked him again. This time in the stomach. The air wheezed out of him, and he dropped.

Gracelyn bolted out of the SUV, and she started running as if her life depended on it.

Because it did.

Chapter Sixteen

Everything inside Ruston was a tight tangle of nerves and adrenaline. He'd been in high-stakes situations before, one of those with Gracelyn, but that had been different. She'd been armed then, and they'd been together. Now she was alone, hurt and with a thug who'd kill her in a blink.

And he'd taken her to the baby farm.

Ruston didn't want to think about what kind of mental torture that was for her. He didn't want to think about what her captor might be doing to her either. That would only shatter what little focus he had, and right now, that focus was what he needed to get to her in time.

He used the hands-free system while he sped down the road, and he called Duncan. "Where are you?" Duncan immediately asked.

"I got a call from the man who's got Gracelyn. He's taking her to the baby farm."

Ruston heard Duncan slam on his brakes. He was obviously changing directions as well, and since he didn't ask for the address, it meant he already knew the location. Then again, just about everyone in local law enforcement did.

"Did you recognize the guy's voice?" Duncan asked.

"No, because he was using a voice distorter," Ruston was quick to say. "He wants the username and password that Zimmer had tatted on him. He says I'm to come alone or Gracelyn will die."

Of course, Ruston knew the plan would be to kill both Gracelyn and him once he had what he wanted. Ruston had to figure out a way, fast, to make sure that didn't happen.

"How the hell did that...?" Duncan started, but he stopped and cursed. "Zimmer might have told someone about the tats, someone who then passed along that info to the killer. Or else the ME's office has a leak," he concluded.

Either was possible, but Zimmer didn't seem as if he trusted anyone enough to share that kind of info. But Ruston immediately rethought that. He could have trusted Tony or Charla. Especially Charla since he'd been her confidential informant.

"I'm guessing the ME filed a report," Ruston said, "and it was either hacked or accessed."

The hacking would point to Devin. The accessing to either Charla or Tony. Which meant they still couldn't use this to confirm the identity of the killer. But Zimmer had likely known that, or had had such strong suspicions, anyway, that he'd then put in that file.

"I can text you the username and password," Duncan said, the hesitation coating his voice. "But we don't know what's in that file yet. Heck, we don't even know where the file's been stored. The techs say it's like looking for a tiny needle in a massive cyber haystack."

"I'm guessing the killer knows that," Ruston concluded. "So, he could have knowledge of where the file is. Maybe he got that from something he found when he killed Zimmer."

Maybe, though, the killer would have to do the same search of that cyber haystack as the tech guys. If so, it'd be a race to see who got there first. If the killer did, then he'd certainly erase everything. But all of that would take time.

Time that Gracelyn didn't have.

"I'm about three miles out from the baby farm," Ruston explained. "Once I'm closer, I'll turn off my headlights. They'll know I'm coming and will be looking for me, but I'm hoping to get close, park and then go on foot."

Duncan cursed again. "I'm at least five miles out. I would ask you to wait for me, but I know you won't. I wouldn't if it were Joelle being held."

"I can't wait," Ruston confirmed. "But when you get here, do a silent approach. I don't want to give the killer any excuse to pull the trigger."

"Will do," Duncan confirmed. "I'll text you the username and password after I hang up. Be careful, Ruston."

"I will." And he would. But that might not be nearly enough. "You, too."

Ruston ended the call and had to slow down to take the final turn toward the baby farm. He drove way too fast on the poor excuse for a road, and as he'd told Duncan, he turned off his headlights when he was about a half mile out. That certainly didn't make driving any easier, but at least there was a moon tonight, and the meager light might stop him from running off the road.

Might.

He rethought that when he hit a deep pothole, and he had to grapple with the steering wheel to stay out of the deep ditches that were on both sides of him.

And that was when he saw it.

The movement from the corner of his eye. Someone running, not on the road but through the grassy area adjacent to it.

His heart crashed against his ribs when he realized it was Gracelyn. Her hands were cuffed in front of her, and she was firing glances behind her. Someone was chasing her.

Since there was no way he could drive to her, Ruston

stopped and got out. He couldn't call out to her because he didn't want to alert the killer to their positions. Instead, Ruston jumped over the ditch and started toward her.

He knew the exact moment when she spotted him. Her head whipped up, and she changed directions. She ran to him.

She didn't get far before a shot rang out.

Ruston felt the slam of fear. The fresh adrenaline. The need to get to Gracelyn now, now, now. If the bullet had hit her, she hadn't gone down. She was still running, and he quickly ate up the distance between them. Ruston immediately took hold of her and dragged her to the ground.

Just as another shot slammed into the dirt a few feet from them.

Ruston followed the direction of the shot and saw the gunman. He had his gas mask shoved up on his head, giving Ruston a look at his face. He didn't recognize him, which meant this was a hired gun.

The thug was trying to take aim while he was running. That was probably why he'd missed with the other two shots. That wouldn't last, though. He'd soon stop, and then Gracelyn and he would be way too easy targets.

"Stay down and let's move," Ruston instructed. He wanted to pull her into his arms, wanted to tell her...so many things. But that was going to have to wait. Maybe he'd get the chance to say those things when this was over.

A third shot came. And a fourth. All too close but still thankfully not hitting the intended mark.

The moment Ruston reached the ditch, he dropped down into it with Gracelyn. It was about three feet deep, so they crouched down, but Ruston knew they couldn't stay this way. The gunman would almost certainly be coming for them, and if he managed to approach at the right angle,

Gracelyn and he wouldn't be able to see the guy until it was too late.

Ruston quickly took out his small pocketknife so he could cut the cuffs from Gracelyn's wrists. It twisted away at him to see that blood on her forehead, but she didn't seem to be in pain. Like him, she was firing glances at the rim of the ditch, watching for the gunman.

The second he'd removed the cuffs, he took out his backup weapon and handed it to her. Then he peered over the top of the ditch. He braced for a shot to be fired at him. But it didn't come.

And the gunman was nowhere in sight.

Hell.

Where had he gone? There were some wild shrubs, and he could have ducked behind one of those. It was too much to hope that he'd just run off.

He saw some movement from a high patch of grass that was about five yards away, and Ruston turned in that direction so he could take aim. And he waited. Watched. Listened. Knowing that Gracelyn was doing the same thing.

There was a soft clicking sound, and he was pretty sure it came from the same grassy area. Moments later, a cloud of white smoke spewed out into the air.

More tear gas.

It wouldn't have the same potent effect as it had inside the hospital, but it could be just as dangerous, considering it was coming right at Gracelyn and him. Once the gas got to their eyes and throats, they wouldn't be able to defend themselves.

"Stay low and move down the ditch," Ruston whispered.

There was a huge disadvantage to that since the thug would be behind him. He'd no doubt be wearing a mask and could use the cloud of gas to conceal himself until he was right on them.

They moved, not as fast as he wanted, but Gracelyn and he scrambled away from the gas. But even over their movements, he heard another of those clicks. Heard the canister drop into the ditch.

And more tear gas came their way.

The moment the gas hit him, Ruston was right back where he'd been at the hospital. Coughing. Eyes burning. No way to fight back. Gracelyn was ahead of him, and she thankfully kept moving. Ruston tried to do that, too, but he heard another sound. Not the click of a canister being triggered.

The thud of someone dropping down into the ditch behind him.

Before Ruston could even turn, there was more movement. And he felt the barrel of a gun press against the back of his head.

"Cooperate," the man snarled, "or I shoot your woman in the back."

GRACELYN KEPT MOVING. Her eyes were stinging, but she thought she was staying just ahead of the worst of the gas. It wasn't a thick cloud but more of a mist. Added to that, the night breeze was dispersing what there was of it. If Ruston and she could just make it a few more feet, they wouldn't get the worst of it and would be able to defend themselves.

She glanced behind her.

And her heart stopped. It certainly felt like it, anyway.

She saw Ruston, not crouching. He was standing now, and not by choice either. There was a man wearing a gas mask behind him, and he was holding Ruston at gunpoint.

"You both throw down your guns," the guy in the gas mask ordered.

Ruston was coughing, but it wasn't nearly as bad as it had been during the other attack. Gracelyn just wished she could better see Ruston's eyes so she could tell if he'd been hurt. But her own eyes were still stinging, and the moonlight was creating plenty of shadows on his face.

"Guns down now," the thug insisted. "I've got a clear shot of your woman," he added to Ruston.

And he did. All the gunman had to do was aim in her direction and fire. There was nothing she could dart behind for cover, and if she tried to scramble out of the ditch, he'd likely just shoot her.

But why hadn't he just done that already?

And why hadn't he finished off Ruston instead of putting a gun to his head?

Because with both Ruston and her alive, they could be used against each other. Leverage. This snake and his boss had to know that she would cooperate to keep Ruston from being killed and vice versa.

"Last chance," the guy warned them. "Guns down now."

Ruston's Glock slid from his hand and dropped on the ground at his feet. Gracelyn knew what that had cost him, to lose the primary way to defend them. But he'd had no choice.

Neither did she.

Gracelyn dropped her gun as well, but she didn't toss it. She wanted it as close to her as possible. That way, if she got the chance to use it, she wouldn't have to reach that far.

"What now?" Ruston demanded.

"We walk and get the hell away from this gas," he answered right away. "Go to the baby farm. You got somebody there who's anxious to see you."

Gracelyn felt the fresh jolt of adrenaline, and she forced herself not to think of the other attack. Those images weren't going to help her think more clearly, and right now, she had to think. She had to figure a way out of this.

"Out of the ditch," the man ordered. "And remember that part about me shooting one of you? I will, you know. In fact, I'll get paid a bonus, so don't test my patience."

A bonus. She hadn't needed more proof that this was a hired thug, but there it was. Someone—maybe Charla, Tony or Devin—had paid this guy to do the dirty work. That could include murder. In fact, that was no doubt the killer's plan after Ruston spilled the username and password.

The thug shoved Ruston out of the ditch first, following quickly behind him and putting the gun back to Ruston's head. A silent warning for Gracelyn not to try anything. Not yet. But leaving the ditch meant leaving their guns behind, and Ruston wouldn't have a backup weapon on him since he'd given it to her.

But there would be backup.

No way would Duncan let Ruston come here alone. The sheriff was no doubt on his way, but he couldn't just come in with sirens blaring. He'd have to do a silent approach, but hopefully that meant he was making his way to them now.

"You stay ahead of us," the thug told Gracelyn. "And go ahead and put your hands on your head so I can see them."

She did as he said, and they started walking. The air cleared even more as they moved away from the ditch and back on the road. Her eyes were still stinging a little, but she could clearly see the building ahead.

And the shadowy figure that stepped out from it.

Gracelyn couldn't tell who it was, and the person stayed back enough so that she couldn't get a good look at him or her.

"Good," the thug muttered. "The boss is coming out to meet us. Might get home in time to watch the game."

It sickened her that he was being so flippant about this. Then again, she figured the other hired guns had been pretty much the same. Well, maybe not Zimmer. But the one who'd attacked with Zimmer had fired shots at the SUV with Abigail inside, and the two goons in the sheriff's office hadn't seemed to care how many people they killed to get to their targets.

"So, it's just you and the boss," she remarked.

He chuckled. "Honey, I'm the only one the boss needs to finish this."

She thought he was telling the truth. Hoped he was, anyway. She didn't want an army of hired thugs waiting for them.

Gracelyn purposely slowed her steps just a little, not because she wanted to delay facing down the killer. No. She was to the point that she wanted to know the person responsible. But she slowed down so that she could try to get closer to Ruston. If the thug was right, this was a two-on-two situation, and while Ruston and she weren't armed, that didn't mean they were defenseless. If they couldn't stall the killer until backup arrived, then they might have to fight their way out of here.

Again.

"And before either of you think about running again," the gunman went on, "my orders are, I lose you two, then I'm to go after the kid."

Oh, the anger came. Boiling hot. A full rage that Gracelyn had to fight to tamp down before she turned and clawed out this snake's eyes. How dare he threaten that little baby. And he was going to pay for that threat. She wasn't sure how, but he would pay.

So would the piece of slime that was waiting for them.

"Glad you could come," the killer said.

And he stepped out so Gracelyn could finally see his face.

DEVIN WAS SMILING when he walked toward them.

Smiling and gloating.

Ruston intended to make sure Devin didn't have those reactions for long. The goon's threats to Gracelyn and Abigail had been more than enough to fuel Ruston's anger, and it had seethed and soared with each step toward this miserable person in this miserable place.

Devin was armed, of course. He had a SIG Sauer in both hands, which he probably thought made him look like a cool bad guy.

"The Green Eagle," Ruston said like a mock greeting.

Devin shrugged. "I'm not going to come out and admit that," he said. "I mean, since I'd be incriminating myself. Oops." He laughed. "I guess I just did. There goes some of my bargaining power." Using the guns, he put those last two words in air quotes.

"Your plan was to tell me that you'd let Gracelyn live if I gave you what you wanted," Ruston spelled out for him.

"Why, yes." There it was again, that smugness that only fueled Ruston's anger. "But you would have never fallen for that anyway. Gracelyn wouldn't have either. You both know how this has to end."

"Yeah, you eliminate everyone who can put you in a cage," Gracelyn muttered.

"True. And so far, so good," he bragged.

Ruston wished he could have disputed that, but with the exception of this lone gunman, the others were dead. Marty, Simon, Archie and three hired guns. There were likely others who had been silenced in the aftermath of the baby farm.

"So far, so good," Devin repeated. "And that's why I need the info that Zimmer left behind."

"How did you know about it?" Ruston asked, shifting his weight so he'd be able to either drop down or lunge at Devin. Ahead of him, Ruston could see Gracelyn doing the same thing.

"Computer leaks," Devin admitted. "The ME isn't very careful about what he puts in his reports. He mentioned the tats, but he didn't give specifics." He paused. "I want specifics. Oh, wait. You need a reason to give it to me. How about a quick, easy death for Gracelyn? As opposed to me making it very, very painful."

"Your hired gun said you would go after Abigail," Gracelyn said, and Ruston heard the razor edge in her voice.

Again, Devin shrugged. "Only as a last resort."

Ruston saw the lie on Devin's face. Devin wouldn't come out now and say that he had planned on taking the baby all along because he probably hadn't wanted to give Gracelyn and Ruston a reason to stay alive.

A reason to fight.

But Gracelyn and he already had that reason. They both loved Abigail, and if they literally rolled over and died, it would leave the baby at the mercy of this monster. That wasn't going to happen.

"You were going to kidnap and sell your own daughter," Gracelyn spit out. "Or maybe she isn't yours."

"She is," Devin verified. "Allie brought me a sample of her DNA because she wanted to prove that I was the father. I'm not sure why she thought it was so important to prove, because I didn't give a rat. Still don't."

Ruston was glad Gracelyn was keeping Devin talking. Anything to distract him. Anything to buy them some time.

And right now, he needed a weapon.

"You didn't kill Allie, though," Gracelyn pointed out. "Is she still a loose end?"

He laughed. "Your sister knows nothing, but I figured I could use her in a roundabout way to get the baby. I mean, if Allie ends up in jail, then I get custody. After I prove paternity, that is, and I can prove it. So can you now that the good sheriff took my DNA. He probably did that, hoping to find something to incriminate me, but the only thing that DNA will prove is that I have a legal right to my biological child."

A child he'd end up selling first chance he got.

And that wasn't all the dirty dealings this SOB had done.

"You're the one who blew our covers," Ruston snapped. "How did you even know we were cops?"

Devin shrugged as if that were nothing. No big deal that Gracelyn and he had nearly died. "I make a habit of using a hacker to check out anyone and everyone I do business with. A hacker who breaks many rules to tap into things like police databases and such." He narrowed his eyes at them. "If you two had died then and there, I wouldn't have to be going through this mess right now."

Ruston was already fuming, but that only added to the flames. He glanced around for something, anything, he could use to fight back. There wasn't anything, which meant he was going to have to do this with his bare hands. He was gearing up to ram his elbow into the thug's gut when there was a flash of headlights. They cut through the darkness at the end of the road and then disappeared.

Both Devin and the thug glanced in that direction.

And Ruston made his move.

With the thug's slight shift of his body, Ruston went for a more direct attack. He turned and slammed his fist into the guy's face. He heard the satisfying sound of cartilage breaking. Blood spewed, and the man howled.

From the corner of his eye, Ruston saw Gracelyn dive toward Devin's legs, tackling him and knocking him back against the building. Ruston cursed, though, when he saw that Devin had managed to hang on to both his guns, but the disadvantage of that was it didn't free up his hands to fight back. Then again, he wouldn't need to actually fight if he could get off a shot.

He did.

The blast tore through the air, the sound tearing through Ruston, and he was terrified that Gracelyn had just been shot. He latched on to the still-howling, still-bleeding thug and dragged him in front of him.

Just in time.

Because there was another shot, and Devin had aimed this one at Ruston. But the bullet meant for him slammed into the thug's chest. He dropped like a stone, giving Devin a clear path to shoot Ruston.

But Gracelyn stopped that from happening.

She kicked the gun from Devin's right hand and sent it flying. Devin pulled the trigger of the second gun, but it was a wild shot that didn't come anywhere near Ruston or her. Thank God. However, Devin immediately tried to shift the weapon to his right hand.

And worse.

During the shift, he bashed Gracelyn on the head, knocking her away from him.

Everything seemed to shift to slow motion. Even the sound of Gracelyn's voice yelling to him, "Get down."

Ruston did get down. He dived to the ground, scooping up

the thug's gun, and the second he had hold of it, he took aim. Even though she was clearly dazed from the blow, Gracelyn scurried away from Devin, giving Ruston a clear shot.

Which he took.

It seemed as if Devin and he pulled the triggers in that same heartbeat of time. Devin missed.

Ruston didn't.

He double tapped the trigger and sent two shots directly into Devin's chest. Devin froze, the shock registering on his face as his gun slid from his hand. Then he flashed that cocky smile one last time before he took in his dying breath.

Gracelyn's gaze connected with Ruston's. For just a second. And they moved. She toward the thug and Ruston toward Devin. Both of them checked to make sure killer and henchman were truly finished.

"He's dead," Ruston verified after touching his fingers to Devin's neck.

"He is, too," Gracelyn confirmed. She stared down at the goon, and her face tightened. She cursed the dead monster.

"Are you all right?" someone called out.

Ruston automatically took aim a split second before he realized it was Duncan. He was on foot, and he was running up the road toward them.

"We're alive," Ruston settled for saying. "But Devin and his hired gun aren't."

Ruston considered calling that in, but it appeared Duncan was already doing that. Instead, Ruston focused on Gracelyn. In addition to the blood on the side of her head, she had a nasty bruise on her face from where Devin had hit her.

Seeing that made him want to go after Devin all over again, but he pulled her into his arms. And held her.

"They were going after Abigail," she muttered. "They were going to kill us and go after her."

"Yeah," he managed to say through the vised muscles in his throat.

Gracelyn's head whipped up, and she looked him straight in the eyes. "We need to check on her. We need to make sure Abigail is okay."

Ruston didn't argue. They started running toward Duncan and the cruiser.

Chapter Seventeen

Gracelyn felt both exhausted and pumped up as if every nerve in her body was on high alert. And on the verge of crashing. Her mind was a tangle of thoughts and fears as Ruston sped toward his family's ranch.

It'd been nearly a half hour since the shoot-out with Devin. Time when they'd had to wait for backup to arrive so that Duncan wouldn't be left at the crime scene alone. During those thirty minutes, Gracelyn had spoken with Joelle not once but twice, and Joelle had assured her that all was well, that no one had come for Abigail. Gracelyn believed her, but she wouldn't breathe easier until she saw the baby for herself.

The moment Woodrow and Luca had arrived, Ruston and she had left, and she'd gotten one last glance of the baby farm in the rearview mirror. Despite nearly being killed there tonight, it no longer held that bogeyman fear for her. It was just a place that bad people had used to do bad things.

And now the leader of those bad people was dead.

Gracelyn didn't feel a drop of grief about that. Just the opposite. A monster was dead, and his death made the world a safer place. Devin wouldn't be around to hire any more henchmen. Wouldn't be around to try to kidnap and sell babies.

"I would suggest you go to the hospital for those injuries," Ruston said, "but I'm guessing you'd rather have an EMT come out to the ranch and examine you."

"The EMT," she immediately agreed. "And you should be checked out, too. We both got some heavy hits of tear gas tonight."

Ruston made a sound of agreement and glanced at her. "How are you, really?"

She did a quick assessment. Her head was hurting, but it wasn't a throbbing pain. "I'm okay enough. How about you?"

"Okay enough," he repeated, and he reached over, took her hand and gave it a gentle squeeze. "I thought I was going to lose you."

There was plenty of emotion in his voice, and she thought they were on the same emotional wavelength here. Well, maybe they were. She had been terrified when she'd thought she would lose Ruston. But there had been an extra layer to that terror.

That she might lose him before she even got the chance to tell him how she felt about him.

She was in love with him.

Gracelyn nearly blurted that out now, but Ruston's phone rang, and she saw Slater's name pop up on the dash screen. All her fears about Abigail came rushing back. It must have been the same for Ruston, because he answered it right away on speaker.

"Nothing's wrong here," Slater said right off the bat. "Abigail is fine."

Gracelyn's breath of relief came out like a loud moan. Ruston did his own version of a breath of relief by muttering something she didn't catch.

"How far out are you?" Slater asked.

"About fifteen minutes," Ruston answered. "Thirteen," he amended when he sped up. Good. The sooner they got there, the better.

Slater made a sound to indicate he was pleased about the shorter arrival time as well. "I thought Gracelyn would want to know that Allie came out of surgery, and she's critical but stable."

Gracelyn had to fight through the fatigue to try to process that. Unlike Devin, she didn't wish her sister dead. Yes, Allie had done some horrible things, but she didn't deserve to die.

"When Allie came out of the anesthesia," Slater went on, "she asked the doctor to give Gracelyn a message."

Everything inside Gracelyn went still. And she waited for Slater to finish. Her sister had done so many reckless, dangerous things that Gracelyn wasn't sure what kind of message she'd want to have passed on to her.

"Allie said that Abigail is yours, Gracelyn, that she'll sign over custody to you," Slater spelled out. "She also won't fight going to prison either."

It took a moment for that to sink in. A long moment where her stomach unclenched. Where so many of her nerves settled.

Abigail was hers.

"Why the change of heart for Allie?" Ruston asked.

"I think nearly dying must have given her some clarity," Slater suggested.

Yes, Gracelyn knew all about that. Being near death did have a way of pinpointing everything. Of making you see what was important.

She certainly had.

And Abigail and Ruston were at the very top of her list of important things.

"I alerted SAPD about Allie coming out of surgery," Slater went on a moment later. "Duncan agreed that they'll be the ones charging her. Conspiracy to kidnapping, human trafficking, obstruction of justice, child endangerment and accessory to attempted murder, including the attempted murder of a police officer. The last two are because she was involved in hiring Zimmer and Robert Radley, who attacked you at Gracelyn's place."

Gracelyn mentally repeated all those charges. With Devin dead, Allie wouldn't have any bargaining power for a deal, which meant she would likely spend the rest of her life in prison.

"See you in a few minutes," Slater said, ending the call.

Ruston gave her hand another gentle squeeze and then brought it to his mouth and brushed a kiss on her fingers. "Are you okay?"

She sighed. "Part of me aches for my sister, but this means Allie won't be able to endanger Abigail again."

Ruston nodded, kissed her hand again. She wished the kiss had been on her mouth. While he'd been holding her. She needed that right now.

She needed him.

Soon, she wanted to tell him that, but for now, she sat in silence, mourning the loss of a sister. Yes, Allie had done some unforgivable things, but she'd also given her the greatest gift. Abigail.

Ruston took the final turn to the ranch, and Gracelyn pushed aside her thoughts to prepare herself for what felt like a homecoming.

She was pleased when she spotted the still-armed ranch hands at the end of the road. Standing guard. Keeping Abigail safe. Gracelyn would owe them all a deep gratitude that she'd never be able to repay. The same was true for Duncan, his deputies, Ruston and his family.

Ruston pulled to a stop in front of the house, and Gracelyn hurried out of the cruiser. Slater was already opening the door before she reached it.

"Uh, are you sure you're okay?" Slater asked when he saw her face.

She nodded, though Gracelyn figured she looked pretty bad for him to have that reaction. However, that was yet something else she'd put on the back burner. For now, she raced up the stairs and straight to the guest room. Carmen and Joelle were both there.

And so was Abigail.

She was sleeping, but Gracelyn picked her up anyway and held her close. The tears came. The tears she'd fought so hard to hold back. But there was no holding back now. Abigail was safe. She was also a little riled at being awakened, and she let out a protesting wail that made Gracelyn smile. She hadn't given birth to Abigail, but this child was hers in every sense of the word.

Gracelyn kissed her cheek and looked back at Ruston when he stepped into the room. He went to them, sliding his arm around Gracelyn's waist and delivering his own kiss to the baby's cheek. Abigail immediately stopped her fussing and smiled at him.

"You've already charmed her," Gracelyn muttered.

"One down, one to go," he muttered back.

Their gazes met for a moment, and Gracelyn saw the love. Well, maybe that was what it was. Love for Abigail, anyway, but what had he meant?

His phone rang, and she saw Duncan's name on the screen. Since Gracelyn wanted to hear what he had to say, she eased the baby back in the crib, thanked both Joelle and Carmen and then stepped out into the hall with Ruston.

"You two back at the ranch yet?" Duncan immediately asked.

"We are," Ruston answered. "Just a couple of minutes ago. Slater filled us in on Allie."

Duncan sighed. "Yeah," he muttered like an apology that Gracelyn knew was meant for her. "I have some good news," he added. "The techs located Zimmer's online file."

Gracelyn saw the surprise flash through Ruston's eyes. "How? They said it'd be a needle in a haystack."

"It would have been, but Zimmer had a clue to the storage site in the password, so the techs were able to narrow it down. They not only found the file, but they were also able to access it."

Something Devin would have certainly been able to do had he gotten the username and password.

"The file is huge and filled with photos and details that would have apparently gotten Devin the death penalty," Duncan explained. "Zimmer confirms that Devin was Green Eagle. And there are other names of people involved in the baby farm, people who probably thought they'd escaped justice."

"Are Tony or Charla on the list?" Gracelyn asked.

"No," Duncan was quick to say.

Gracelyn felt nothing but relief about that. Yes, she would apologize to Charla and Tony for believing they were guilty, and she was glad they hadn't been dirty cops.

"Archie, Marty and Simon were on the list," Duncan went on, "and that explains why Devin had them murdered. Devin was basically eliminating anyone who could link him to the baby farm."

Yes, that made sense. It was the reason Devin wanted to

eliminate Ruston and her, too. And Allie. But maybe he'd let her live, with the hopes that she would end up taking the blame for not only the attacks and murders but also for the baby farm itself. Gracelyn could see Devin trying to use Allie as the ultimate scapegoat.

"I'll be tied up here a while longer, but I'm hoping to be home in about two hours," Duncan added. "Is everything and everyone okay there?"

"Yes," Ruston and Gracelyn muttered in unison, and for the first time in nearly a year, Gracelyn could say that was the truth.

She was okay.

The past would always be with her, but it wasn't the past she was looking at now. She was looking at a future.

Gracelyn was looking at Ruston.

And he was looking at her.

He ended the call, slipped his phone into his pocket and immediately pulled her into his arms. He took her mouth in a deep kiss that notched up her "okay" to something much, much more.

But how much more?

What she said in the next few minutes could change everything, but Ruston might not be ready to hear it. Still, she needed to tell him what she'd been holding inside. And she would. As soon as he finished melting her with this kiss.

When he'd left her breathless and on cloud nine, he eased back from her and flashed that incredible smile again.

"I'm in love with you," she said. Gracelyn braced herself for the shock. Maybe for him to back away and tell her that he needed more time.

That didn't happen.

Ruston kissed her again, and this one was so hot that

Gracelyn wasn't sure how she managed to stay on her feet. The man had a way of firing up every inch of her.

"Good." He muttered that single word while his mouth was still against hers.

But he added more words to it.

"Because you and I are of a like mind here," he went on. "Because I'm in love with you, too."

Now she didn't stay on her feet. Or at least she wouldn't have if Ruston hadn't caught her. Her heart filled with so much emotion. Not the bad ones this time either. All the very best ones. Happiness. Need. And love. So much love.

But Ruston added to that, too.

"I say, since we both love Abigail, that we raise her together," he threw out there. "What do you think about that?"

"I think it's perfect," she managed to say.

And it was just that. Perfect. Still, Ruston managed to add to that, too. Because he pulled her back to him for a long, slow kiss.

* * * * *

USA TODAY bestselling author Delores Fossen's miniseries Saddle Ridge Justice continues next month with Tracking Down the Lawman's Son. *And if you missed the first book in the series, look for* The Sheriff's Baby, *available now wherever Harlequin Intrigue books are sold!*

HARLEQUIN
Reader Service

Enjoyed your book?

Try the perfect subscription for Romance readers and get more great books like this delivered right to your door.

See why over 10+ million readers have tried Harlequin Reader Service.

Start with a Free Welcome Collection with free books and a gift—valued over $20.

Choose any series in print or ebook.
See website for details and order today:

TryReaderService.com/subscriptions